# Readers love
# DIRK GREYSON

## *Flight or Fight*

"I recommend this to those who love a good murder mystery, who love digging nuggets of truth out of murky waters, who adore characters that have got spark, and endings that are perfect."

—MM Good Book Reviews

"Dirk Greyson brings us a well plotted murder mystery with non-stop suspense and action."

—The Novel Approach

## *Dawn and Dusk*

"This is a must read for any that love romance that's worked for, mystery and suspense, and two men that love hard, sex hard, and carry guns."

—House Millar

"I really enjoy this series."

—The Blogger Girls

## *Darkness Threatening*

"…a worthy follow-up and a fabulous HEA…"

—Prism Book Alliance

By DIRK GREYSON


An Assassin's Holiday
Flight or Fight
Playing With Fire

DAY AND KNIGHT
Day and Knight
Sun and Shadow
Dawn and Dusk

YELLOWSTONE WOLVES
Challenge the Darkness
Darkness Threatening


Published by DREAMSPINNER PRESS
www.dreamspinnerpress.com

# PLAYING WITH FIRE

## DIRK GREYSON

Published by
DREAMSPINNER PRESS

5032 Capital Circle SW, Suite 2, PMB# 279, Tallahassee, FL 32305-7886 USA
www.dreamspinnerpress.com

Playing With Fire
© 2016 Dirk Greyson.

Cover Art
© 2016 L.C. Chase.
http://www.lcchase.com
Cover content is for illustrative purposes only and any person depicted on the cover is a model.

ISBN: 978-1-63477-909-8
Digital ISBN: 978-1-63477-910-4
Library of Congress Control Number: 2016913021
Published November 2016
v. 1.0

Printed in the United States of America

This paper meets the requirements of
ANSI/NISO Z39.48-1992 (Permanence of Paper).

To Lynn, who helped form the idea for this one, and to Dominic, who is now wondering how I know so much about serial killers.

# CHAPTER 1

JIM CRAWFORD groaned as he flipped on the lights to his patrol car, turned around, and raced toward Route 1, which ran down the center of New Cynwood, Pennsylvania. The entire town was on edge, and this was only going to make it worse, much worse. Customers by the droves were staying away from the businesses in town out of fear. He could almost hear his boss screaming at him to do something about this, the council was going to have his hide, and of course, the highly upper-crust town was going to feature in the evening news yet again.

He pulled into the shopping center near where an ambulance was already coming to a stop, parked, and got out, staying clear of the lifesaving personnel. As other officers arrived, he got them busy securing a perimeter.

"What have we got, Tommy?" Jim asked the EMT.

"She's already gone. There's nothing we can do for her," Tommy said, gently covering the body with a sheet. "You may as well call in the coroner and a medical examiner. But it looks exactly like the last one to me."

"I was afraid of that." This was the fourth of these shootings in the last few months, and as he looked around, he spotted the most likely place the shot was taken from.

Jim made the calls and got everyone rolling. "Check the surrounding buildings and get these people out of here. What if the shooter decides to take another shot?" It hadn't happened so far, but who was to say the pattern wouldn't change? In fact, Jim was pretty sure of what they were going to find—a single shell casing, sitting perfectly straight on the ground, exactly from where the shot had been taken, and not a single thing else.

"What is it, Sergeant?" Jim turned when Paul Carson, one of his senior men, approached.

"Found this right up there," he said, pointing to the exact spot Jim had been contemplating.

Shit, it was fucking frightening that he could think like this bastard. The problem was, he could only do that after the shooting took place. Not before the asshole took his shot and ended yet another life.

"We've worked way too many of these. Get statements from everyone. Find out what they heard and saw. Check anyone in or around that building to see if they saw anything unusual. This guy has got to make a mistake, and we need to be there when he does." Jim calmed himself so he could think, refusing to get too wrapped up in this case. He needed to be able to see things clearly if he was going to solve this, and he had to. His career depended on it.

When Carl, the coroner, arrived, Jim let him make his assessment and then waited for whatever information he could give him. "Looks just like the others I have back in the morgue," Carl said softly. "If I had to guess, I'd say it was the same caliber and probably the same rifle, though I can't confirm that until I extract the bullet and test it."

"We already found his calling card." Jim held up the evidence bag and signed it over to Carl so he could match the bullet to the casing.

"Let me get busy, and I'll give you any information I can as quickly as possible."

Jim nodded and turned away so he could finish processing the crime scene. He wasn't about to let it go until he was sure he had everything there was possible to get. "Come with me?" he asked Paul, who nodded, and they went to inspect where the shot had come from.

Like the three previous murders, according to initial reports, there had been a single shot and then someone had fallen to the ground. Just like that, a life had ended. Jim went inside the small, empty office building and up to the roof. Sure enough, the markers were still in place, but the photographs had been taken and the evidence collected and bagged.

"A great vantage point, and it would be hard for someone down there to see up here because they'd be looking into the sun at the time. He picks his places really well."

"He does indeed, Paul." There were things Jim knew about their killer, but so much he didn't. "The guy is methodical, distant, and so far we've not been able to find a single connection between the victims. They seem random, and that's what's got us stumped."

"They do have something in common. All of them took place here, within four blocks. If it isn't the victims that connect them, then maybe it's the place or where he takes his shots," Paul offered.

Jim had thought of that, and they had run down every lead, but after this killing, they were going to have to look at everything again. Sometimes it felt as though they were running in circles, but it had to be done to ensure nothing was missed.

He watched the area from the shooter's point of view, then let the guys finish up and headed back down. He listened to witnesses and reviewed the statements with the other officers, but like the cases before, no one had seen anything until the shot was fired, and then all eyes had been on the victim.

"Anything new to report?" Captain Westin asked as he strode toward Jim. These shootings were getting on everyone's nerves, and a lack of progress made everyone edgy.

"I wish. It's the same as the others," Jim said rather softly. "This guy leaves us almost nothing to go on. Not even a footprint in the roofing material. Just that single bullet casing to taunt us." He groaned. "I'm going to work the evidence, and then I think we need some help."

"I don't want to call in the feds, but...."

Jim moved away from the others to ensure privacy. "No, Cap, I mean the only way we're going to catch this guy is to find someone who can think like him. This isn't someone we're going to catch using our normal methods because I think he's well aware of what we do, how we do it, and the way we'll try to catch him."

"What do you propose?"

"I'm not sure exactly. Let me finish up here, and then can we talk about it in your office?" He really needed some time to clarify his thoughts before he requested money for his proposal.

"Definitely," Captain Westin said, and Jim returned to finishing up with the crime scene.

Once he felt confident he could release it, Jim headed back to the station, where he instructed all of his officers to get the statements reviewed, typed up, and sent within the next hour. He had to have all of it so he could look for any differences from the previous scenes.

With instructions handed out, he sat at his desk and made a phone call. "Marilyn," he said when she answered, and his stomach did a little flip. "It's Jim Crawford." He hadn't talked to her in nearly two years, and as much as he didn't want to open this door, it was something he felt he had to do.

"Jimmy," she said happily. "I thought you'd fallen off the face of the earth. I knew when you and Garrett split up that things would change, but you know you can call and talk if you want. We were friends, you know." She sounded pissed, and Jim regretted pulling away from a lot of their mutual friends when things went south with Garrett. It had been easier than trying to figure out which friends he'd gotten in the separation. Marilyn had been a hard one because he'd always gotten along with her really well, but she and Garrett had been colleagues and in the same discipline.

"Things were difficult for a long time." That was the only explanation he had that made any sense at all once he vocalized it.

"I know that, and I'm still a little angry at him." She paused, and he heard a door close in the background. "He wasn't the only one who got left behind."

That was news to him.

"I'm guessing you didn't call to hash out ancient history."

"No. But I will call more often, I promise. I miss you and Brian." Hell, when Garrett left, so had almost all of his social life.

"So, what do you need? Are you still with Philly PD?"

"No. I moved to New Cynwood a few months after the breakup. It was easier and a great opportunity." He grabbed some papers off his desk. "I'm working the shootings."

"God, I saw those on the news. They're awful."

"They are, and we need some help. You're plugged in there, and I'm hoping you can point me to an expert on psychological criminal behavior."

She chuckled. "A criminological psychologist?"

"Yes. One of those. Is there someone you can recommend? I could really use some insight."

"All right. Let me look into it a little. We're pretty siloed here, as most educational institutions of our size are, but I happen to have some contacts in the psych department and I can make a few calls. Will you give me a number where I can reach you?" After he rattled off his direct line, she said, "I'll call back as soon as I can."

"Thanks." Jim hung up and thanked all that was holy that Marilyn understood urgency, at least in this situation. Sometimes she took her own time with things. He also thanked his stars that Marilyn didn't seem to hate him for not calling for all this time. Heck, she even seemed to understand, at least to a degree—something even he didn't all the time. Things with Garrett had been good, until they'd gone bad, and he was still trying to figure all that shit out after two fucking years.

"Crawford," Captain Westin snapped, and Jim stood and followed him into the office. "Okay, what is it you want? The township is about to explode, and we have to solve this fast. This has gone on too long, and people are scared shitless."

That was like the understatement of the decade.

"I'm working on a criminal psychologist. They work with criminals and people with pathological and psychotic personalities. I think we need someone who can get into this guy's head. We have data on his behavior and the crimes committed, but we aren't sure how to use it."

"You mean like *The Mentalist* or something?" Captain Westin asked skeptically. "You know that's just made up for television."

"Yeah. But it is a real discipline, and we need the help. It's either that or lose control of the case, and with each incident, we get closer to that. So how much can I offer?" He wasn't going to pull any punches. They needed help, he knew it, and from the doubt in the captain's eyes, he knew it as well.

"Whatever the fuck he wants. At this point I can get the money for just about anything if it will help solve this damn case. Now get out, find one of these patho people, do it fast, and get some results—or else they're going to be calling for both our heads." He glared at Jim, who took that as the end of their meeting, so he left the office and returned to his desk as his phone rang.

"How fast can you get down here?" Marilyn said without preamble. "I think I have just the guy for you. But...."

"What? It isn't Garrett, is it?"

"God, no. He's ancient philosophy. I doubt he'd be able to help you. No, I have one of the leading experts of psychological criminal behavior, and he's agreed to meet with you, but he has appointments for the next few hours and then class after that."

"Did you tell him how important this is?" Jim asked as he grabbed his things. "Surely his other appointments can't be life or death."

"Just come down here. Barty Halloran is someone you have to meet to believe. Call me when you're close, and I'll meet you and lead you over."

Once he agreed, Jim got a move on.

To say traffic was hell was an understatement. It took an hour on the Schuylkill to get downtown. He thought of turning on his lights, but he wasn't on an emergency call, so he inched along and waited to get downtown. He did use his official vehicle to get a parking spot, then called Marilyn, who met him in the center of the urban campus. She was a tiny, thin woman with a smile as huge as all outdoors.

"You look great," Jim said as she approached and hugged him tight.

"I'm so mad at you for not calling. Just because Garrett was an ass doesn't mean you have to cut everyone out of your life." She released him and was already moving. "I'd love to catch up, but we have little more than half an hour for you to meet Barty."

"Okay." He followed behind as she led him into a relatively modern, completely nondescript brick building and up the stairs to the third floor. The place seemed to have been designed with a lack of character and a great deal of blandness in mind, like they wanted to stifle creative thought rather than encourage it.

"His office is right up here," Marilyn said without slowing down. She reached the door she wanted, knocked, and then opened it.

"Do I know you?" the almost beanpole man inside asked, staring at Marilyn a little blankly.

"I'm Marilyn Grove. We spoke on the phone." She smiled, but he didn't.

"Yes." The man turned to the clock on his desk and then back, his gaze landing on Jim, who swallowed. His blue eyes were the color of ice and held a slight chill.

"I'm Jim Crawford, a detective with the New Cynwood Police Department, and I'm working a case that could use some of your expertise."

"Dr. Bartholomew Halloran. You can call me Barty." He motioned to the chair.

"I'll leave you to talk," Marilyn said, and somehow Jim felt as though he were being thrown to the wolves. She turned and left, her footsteps echoing down the hallway.

Barty closed the door and sat at his desk, looking at him. "Well?" He blinked a few times behind his black-rimmed glasses. "You need my help," he said, sounding confused.

"Yes. You might have heard about the shootings we've had."

"Of course. I've been fascinated by them."

Jim wondered at the words chosen. "How so?"

"Of course there are many things I don't know, but the perpetrator seems like he'd make an interesting case study for my research." Barty sat still, watching him, and Jim wondered if he was trying to get into his head somehow. It was a little creepy the way Barty seemed to look deeply into his eyes, but showed nearly nothing in his.

"We have few clues as to who this person is, and with four deaths now, I thought we needed more insight. Someone who can help us get into the mind of the killer to figure out how he thinks and maybe find a way to catch him before he kills again."

Barty nodded. "You are correct in assuming your killer is male. Men kill from a distance and are detached. Women usually kill more close up and it's personal... crimes of passion and so on." He turned back to the desk, and Jim thought he was checking his clock again. "I have an appointment shortly that I can't miss."

Jim didn't want to pressure the guy, but he was becoming agitated. "Do you understand how important this is? People have died, and more will die unless we can stop him."

"I'm aware of that, and I can try to help you." Barty turned slightly and checked his computer. "I have appointments for the next few hours that are too late to reschedule." He made a humming noise in his throat. "I can start tomorrow morning if that's okay with you. I think this could be very fascinating and really advance my work."

"It could also save lives," Jim said. Barty was certainly as strange as Marilyn hinted at.

"I understand that's important—of course it is." Barty sounded as though the words were something he'd learned rather than truly felt. "Sometimes in my line of work, we have to look at deeply emotional and frightening things in a very dispassionate way in order to arrive at conclusions and knowledge that helps us understand why people do the evil things they do to one another."

Jim could understand that, and yet there was something about Barty that made him wonder if he was the guy Jim was looking for. "Do you really think you can help?"

"I believe so."

Confidence Jim understood, and it eased some of his growing doubts.

"I'm very good at what I do—one of the best, I believe—and I'm sure I can help you."

"How can you be so sure?"

"I don't have all the facts, but from what I've read, I'd say you've come to the conclusion that the killer is choosing victims at random, is remote, and is trying to send some sort of message, but you aren't able to figure out what that message is. The thing is, he may not want you to understand the message because it isn't intended for you, but for whoever or whatever the trigger is that started his rampage. And yes, there is a trigger of some sort, I'm sure of it." Barty said all of this dispassionately. "I'm assuming that you've gone over all the physical evidence. What I'll do is try to build a profile of the killer and see if I can figure out why he's killing."

"I'd appreciate that." He had to admit that those were the same things he had been thinking.

"I'd also go on to say that your killer is smart and methodical, judging by the lack of evidence. It's difficult and takes planning to not leave behind anything of yourself at a crime scene. But I get the feeling there's more to it than that. I'd need to look deeper to be able to come up with a next move."

"All right. Then I'll see you tomorrow at the station." Jim handed Barty one of his cards. "I'll be there by seven."

"That late? I get up at five thirty and can be there by six. That way I'll miss the traffic."

"All right, six," Jim said. This case was going to require extra hours, so they might as well get started. He just hadn't expected Barty to want to get there that early. "I'll see you then, and we'll have everything we have available to you. But...."

"Yes, I know. This is confidential, and I mustn't speak with anyone about it." Barty stood and opened the door. Jim walked out, and a young girl—about twenty, with long brown hair in a ponytail—stepped in after him.

"Yes, Carry Ann," Barty said in the same way he'd greeted Jim.

Jim stood off to the side and checked his messages.

"I know my assignment was late, but my mother went into the hospital and I had to help take care of her. She's better now, and I'm caught up, so I'm just asking for a little leniency."

"But you were late, and I told you at the beginning of the semester that I don't accept late work under any circumstances," Barty said as though it were the most logical thing in the world.

"I got everything caught up, and my mother nearly died. It was less than a day, and I sent it to you. I missed class because of it and...." Her voice broke.

"But it was still late," Barty said, clearly confused.

"My mother nearly died...." Carry Ann sniffled, and Jim could almost see the scene in Barty's office.

"The assignment was late, and I clearly told everyone...."

"I work hard, and I participate in class while the others just sit there, and I always do extra work. You know that." She was making a very good case. "Can't you have a heart?"

Jim waited for Barty's answer.

"Of course I could. But this...." Barty stopped, and Jim would have loved to have seen his expression just to learn a little more about him. "All right. I'll accept the assignment this time, but not again. And you must never tell anyone, or else they will all require the same treatment." That confusion was clear in Barty's voice once again, like he didn't understand the need for this conversation in the first place. "I'll return your assignment with the others at our next class."

"Thank you," Carry Ann said with relief, and Jim continued down the hall, feeling bad that he'd listened in while at the same time wondering about what he'd heard. Marilyn was right: meeting Barty Halloran was an experience, and he wondered what working with the cute professor was going to be like.

Jim stopped in his tracks. How in the hell had the word *cute* slipped into his head? He groaned and pushed it aside. He wasn't going to go there, not again. There had been one too many geeky professors in his life already. Jim texted Marilyn, who met him outside the building.

"How did it go with him?" She was smiling slightly.

Jim blinked. "He's… different."

"To say the least. I don't have a great deal of contact with people from other departments, but I've crossed paths with Barty a few times. He's brilliant and completely clueless when it comes to people."

"Like Sheldon on the *Big Bang Theory*?"

Marilyn shook her head. "I don't think so. He just doesn't get other people." She motioned them ahead. "We aren't friends or anything, but Brian and I were at a party with him…." She paused as she thought. "About eighteen months ago, I guess. It was a graduation cocktail party of some sort, and he was there. Stood in the corner the entire time, watching everyone. I'd met him so I went to say hi, and he looked at me like he was lost and didn't quite know what to do. He answered my questions, but he never initiated anything and seemed to feel… relieved once the conversation was over. He's a nice enough man and isn't obnoxious, just clueless when it comes to interactions with others that aren't academic in nature."

"I don't get it. How can a psychology professor not get other people?"

"It's academic. He studies behavior and how others think, but has no tools to interact directly with them. It's like some part of him is missing in a way. Like he never learned how to interact with people socially. Maybe that's why he went into the field he did, so he could try to learn. I don't know. But he's one of those people that you want to know why he does what he does and what makes him tick. Maybe you can figure it out when you work with him."

"Not likely," Jim said. "I mean, he seemed okay, just a little on the strange side. But then again, we're after a killer who shoots people on the street, so maybe it will take a strange guy to find this psycho."

"You never know," Marilyn said with one of her weird smiles. She hugged him again, and Jim had to be careful not to hurt her. She always seemed like she would break in his arms. "Don't be a stranger. Okay?" She stepped away, and Jim hurried to his car and headed back to the station.

He walked into near pandemonium.

"Get in here," Captain Westin said as soon as Jim got to his desk. Officers scurried out of the way as they walked through the station, and Jim closed the door behind him. "I received a message while you were out." He turned his computer monitor around and pressed Play.

"I see you're getting nowhere, and you aren't going to. I can get to anyone at any time." The voice was distorted somehow, so Jim leaned forward. "If you want the shootings to stop, you're going to have to figure out what I want and then give it to me. The best you can hope for is that I'll go back to my life." The recording stopped.

There had been few times in Jim's life when he'd come face-to-face—or, in this case, voice-to-voice—with evil. He'd met plenty of murderers and thieves, but mostly they were crimes of opportunity or passion. This was someone who killed for sport, to send some obscure message.

"Jesus. How was it delivered?"

"To my voice mail. We've already traced the call to a phone that's no longer active. We're trying to trace the call back to a location, but only have a general area."

A knock sounded, and then the door cracked open. "Here's the report you wanted. The phone was sold at a Walmart."

"Find out which store and see if they'll cooperate. We might be able to trace it back through their systems to a purchase date, and then we can see if we get the guy on camera." Jim was hopeful for the first time since this investigation began.

"They can't. They sell these by the hundreds, and they come with a certain number of minutes already on them. There's no activation, and once the minutes are used, they can buy more, but this guy will probably dump it if he hasn't already and just buy another."

"Try to track it anyway until we're sure the trail is dead and cold," Jim said, and Captain Westin agreed, even though the officer was probably right and this was another dead end.

The officer nodded and closed the door behind him.

"Did you have any luck?"

"I have a possible expert coming in tomorrow. A psychology professor from Dutton," Jim said.

"What's he like?"

The first thought that came to his mind was geeky-hot, but he wasn't going to tell his captain that. He liked his job. "Weird."

"How so?"

"I can't describe it. But the guy is a little off in some ways."

"Is he what we need to solve the case?" Captain Westin asked, and Jim thought for a few seconds before nodding slowly.

"He may be exactly what we need." Jim was beginning to wonder. Their killer was a lot of things, and off his nut was definitely one of them. Maybe it took a weird professor to catch a bizarre killer. They definitely had one of those.

"What do you have planned next?"

"I need to get everything together that we have on each killing so I can present it to Barty when he gets here tomorrow morning at six." Jim watched Captain Westin's eyebrows rise. "It seems that's the time he likes to start work."

"Okay, then." The phone rang, and he groaned and motioned Jim out of the office. "This isn't going to be pretty. The mayor's going to chew me out."

Jim left and shut the door as the screaming came through the phone. Why politicians figured yelling at people was going to make things come together faster was beyond him.

As he sat at his desk and woke his computer, Paul Carlson came over. "What can I do to help? I finished getting all of the evidence cataloged and logged into the system, and the statements are coming in."

"Go ahead and organize them. I have some help coming in tomorrow, and I want to get everything together."

"What kind of help?"

Jim looked up from his screen. "That's yet to be seen." He raised his eyebrows, and Paul rolled his eyes and they got to work.

It took hours to gather the evidence and data on the crime scenes. Though it was organized and cataloged, much of the knowledge was in Jim's head, so he did his best to get his thoughts and suspicions down on paper. He also made sure that everything was easily accessible, and then he reviewed the entire case once again just to make sure he hadn't missed any connections.

IT WAS dark and late by the time he left the station. Jim got into his Escape, drove home, and pulled into the house he'd inherited from his grandfather. The thing was a huge pile of stone and Tudor beams, leaded glass windows, and heavy oak doors, surrounded by huge trees and a massive carpet of green. His grandfather had left him the property and a trust to manage and maintain it because it had been Jim's favorite place in the whole world growing up. He still loved it, but a whole lot less now that it was his responsibility, along with the all the contents.

He pulled into the garage and crossed the parklike walk to the back door. He unlocked it, deactivated the alarm, and went inside the huge, otherwise empty house. "Sometimes I expect you to be here to greet me, Grandpa," Jim said. He had to make some noise, or the place would weigh him down. To say it was too big for one person was an understatement. Twelve could live here and rarely see each other, he swore, but didn't intend to find out.

His phone rang as he emptied his pockets and set everything on the counter. Glancing at the display, he girded his loins for whatever onslaught was coming. "Hi, Deidre."

"I heard there was another one today. Have you come to your senses yet and decided to give up this whole Sherlock Holmes thing you have going on and join the rest of us?"

God, she could be a complete witch with a capital *B* sometimes.

"Not all of us can exist in the rarified world of economics," he retorted. "I like my job, and I'm going to catch whoever is doing this. So did you only call to be a pain in the ass, or was there something else? It's late, I'm tired, and I have a huge day tomorrow."

She responded as though the weight of the world rested on her shoulders. "I called because I was promoted a few weeks ago. I'm the new head of the Economics department at Templeton. They announced it a while ago, and Franklin and I are throwing a party to celebrate. It's Sunday afternoon in the backyard of the house. Rain or shine. We'll be having a canopy put up just in case."

The weather certainly should never compromise one of Deidre's social engagements. "Congratulations. I'm happy for you. I'll try to come. Text me the time, and if I can get a few hours away, I'll be there."

That huff came through the line again—one that said the entire world should get out of the way of his younger sister. His parents had spoiled her rotten. Not only was she the only daughter, but the youngest as well, and she was used to getting exactly what she wanted. His parents had more than seen to that.

"It's the best I can do at this point."

"Fine. You know if you got a job befitting your status, you would be able to move in social circles without…."

"Quit being a shit," Jim said in his best police officer tone. "You have no right to act that way, missy, and don't think I'm going to stand for the attitude the way Dad and your husband do. I changed your diapers, and so help me, I can tell all of your so-called society a hell of a lot of things about Deidre Crawford-Grinnell."

"You wouldn't," she said, scandalized.

"Don't try me. I may carry a gun, but you've spent enough time around horses to know that if you spread the manure, eventually you're going to step in it, and I can see to it that it's up to your ears. Now I'll be there if I can, but there are to be no snide comments about my job or my life. You have a pool, and I can still pick you up and throw you in."

She gasped. "Don't you dare!"

"Then don't give me a reason," he countered, and Deidre grew quiet.

"Fine. I know I was bitchy," she said, and Jim waited, tapping his foot and silently counting to three. "Mindy and Meghan were asking if you'd be there, and they asked if they could go for a ride in your police car."

He'd been waiting for her to pull out the big guns, and his nieces were certainly that. Mindy was three and Meghan was four. They were bubbly and precious as all hell. "I'll be there if I can. You saw the news, and this is my case, so I have to solve it. I'm bringing in a professor to help tomorrow."

"Not your ex-whatever...," she said.

"Garrett taught philosophy. He'd be as much help as you would. Hey, just think about it, I could bring you in when we need to interrogate suspects. You could lecture them on economic theory, and they'd confess out of boredom."

"Ass," she countered, but Jim heard a smile in her tone.

"I'll call before Sunday to let you know what's going on."

"Okay. Dress is garden party elegance."

"So the white tuxedo jacket," he said.

"Har-har. Just look really nice. There will be people there you can meet." She ended the call, and Jim had to give her credit—she hung up before he could yell that she was not to try to fix him up with anyone. His family were the kings of social facades and living in denial. He'd had a partner for three years, and Jim had brought Garrett to a number of family functions. They had loved him. Garrett was a professor and looked the part, with his geeky sophistication and charm. Deidre had adored him, and they'd talked for hours about things that went over everyone else's heads. Of course, that had been the point. Feeling superior was also a family trait.

After the split, his family had somehow gotten it into their collective heads that Jim would start dating women. His mother had said, "The whole thing with men was a flop, so you should do what's expected now. You need to marry, have children, and continue the family name and legacy. We were accepting while you were trying to figure things out, but it's time to put all that behind you." She'd glared at him in her blue-and-white Prada suit and from under a pair of sunglasses that would pay most people's mortgage for a month.

Of course Jim had done his best to make her understand, but it seemed to fall on deaf ears. He was the black sheep of his family. Not only was he gay, but he was a police officer as well. "At least become a lawyer if you want to go into the law," his father had said. "You can parlay a law degree into a number of things that will open doors for you."

Jim had ignored it all and followed his own path, wondering if that had been what they truly hated. After all, society was definitely not filled with people who thought for themselves.

Jim opened the freezer, pulled out a frozen dinner, and threw it into the microwave. He also made a small salad and carried his food into the den, closed the door, and turned on the television. After eating, he put his dishes in the dishwasher and then went upstairs and down the almost cavernous hallway to his bedroom.

This was the room he loved most in the house. It had been his grandparents' bedroom, and it overlooked the backyard, with its flower gardens and paths between them, fountains, and everything else his grandmother had loved. Jim paid a fortune to keep it all in working order, and he loved every bit of it, especially on a night like this. He pushed up the window, letting the cool night air and the noise of water from the fountain drift into the room.

Jim leaned on the windowsill, closed his eyes, and let the sound work its way into his soul. Lately he'd felt the damn thing getting blacker and colder as he saw more and more of the dark underbelly of humanity. That had been why he'd come back home to work. New Cynwood was supposed to be safe.

He should have known better.

Turning away, Jim went to his bathroom, stripped off his clothes, and stepped into the shower. He felt better once he'd washed off the grime of his day and then got into bed. This place was his refuge and sanctuary, but lately sleep eluded him each and every night. It had for a while, and long before the shootings had begun. At first he saw Garrett's face in his dreams, when they still had their life together. Those had faded with time and had been replaced by images of the victims being shot on the street. A few times it had been Garrett being shot, and after those nightmares, he'd broken his own rule and called Garrett just to make sure he was truly okay. He hoped tonight would be one of the quiet ones because he desperately needed his sleep.

As he settled down under the crisp, clean sheets, he closed his eyes. Within moments the image of a tall, lanky professor with his shirt buttoned all the way up and black-rimmed glasses came to mind. Jim groaned, punched his pillow, and rolled over, driving the image away.

Damn it. He knew he had a type; hell, he'd always known, even before Garrett—geeky-professor sort, with their slight awkwardness and glasses. They had to have glasses. But he'd been down that road twice. Once just after college, and it had ended, not badly, but out of necessity for him. Jim had been young and had moved on… to Garrett. Garrett had captured his heart, stayed with him for three years, and then left him for greener academic pastures.

"Fuck this shit," Jim said out loud as he rolled over yet again. That path was closed, and he wasn't doing it again.

Jim punched the pillow and forced his mind onto the rippling water outside the window. It was going to be another hellacious night.

# CHAPTER 2

THE ALARM was about to ring, and Barty switched it off. He hated the buzz, and every time it actually sounded, it threw off his day. Of course, most people would ask why he kept it. He hated the thing, so he was always sure to wake up before it. See, there were reasons why he did things, even if the rest of the world didn't understand. Barty was used to that. No one understood him, and they hadn't in quite a few years. Well, if he thought about it, no one had really gotten what things were like in his head, but at least his nana had tried to understand.

"Barty, sometimes you have to put others first," she used to tell him.

"But why?" he'd asked.

"Because it's nice, and because hurting others is bad and we want to be good. And if you're good, then maybe other people will be good to you." She'd told him that over and over again, and Barty had tried to live by that even if he still didn't understand. Finally he'd put it all down to being nice. He could be nice.

"Thanks, Nana," Barty said softly, although the woman was nowhere near to hear, as he got out of the bed to the protest of his bedmate. "Penelope," he said, and she stretched her long, sleek gray body before coming around to rub against him. Of course, he knew it was preparation for the demand for food that was to come later, but Barty loved her motor purr when she wanted attention. He gently stroked her and then got up, put on his robe, and strode out into the other room of his tiny apartment. There were only three if the bathroom counted, but he liked it and it was enough for the two of them.

Barty went through his morning routine like the efficient clockwork it was: starting the coffee, feeding Penelope, brushing his teeth, and cleaning up. Once he was done, he poured his first cup of coffee and went to his bedroom with the cat right behind him. She jumped on the bed and sat down, grooming herself while Barty dressed. Their pattern had only changed the last time Barty had taken her to the vet and she'd

18

had to stay all night. The poor thing had howled the following morning until Barty brought her home, and then she went about the routine like it had never been interrupted.

Once he was dressed, he checked himself in the mirror, not because he particularly cared how he looked, but he didn't want to make a bad impression. "Clothes matter, and you want others to like you," Nana had said, so he took her words to heart.

The last thing he did was make sure Penelope had food and water for the day before picking up his folio. He waited by the door, and Penelope jumped onto the stool he kept there for her. He stroked her twice and got purrs as a reward before leaving the apartment.

Normally Barty bicycled to work whenever he could. It was good for the environment, and it meant he didn't have to brave the city streets in a car. He hated cars with a passion, but he had one and used it when he needed to. That was why he always went in to work so early. Traffic was less, and he could remain stress-free. Barty unlocked his green Escort, got inside, started it, and rolled down the windows to air out the mustiness. Then backed out of his spot and drove to the police station.

He arrived in plenty of time and wished he'd asked Jim where he should park, but he found a spot and got out of the car.

"That's for employees," an officer said as he came out of the building.

Barty looked around and then turned back to the man. "I am one for today, I guess." He walked up to the door the officer had come out of and stopped when he was tapped on the shoulder.

"You need to go to the front." He took Barty by the arm.

"I'm here to see Detective Jim Crawford," Barty said, yanking his arm away. "I'd appreciate it if you kept your hands to yourself. That kind of touching isn't appropriate." He glared at the man as he brushed off his sleeve. "I'm expected." He waited. "Well, are you going to show me where he is?" It was a perfectly logical question, and Barty waited for an answer.

"This way," the officer said, motioning and following Barty as he went farther inside and up the stairs. "Wait right here," the officer said and walked to where Barty saw Jim standing.

Jim motioned him over. "I see you made it." He glanced at the clock and then back at him.

"Yes. You said you would have things for me to look at," Barty said, ready to get right to work.

"I do. Would you like some coffee?" Jim led the way to the coffeemaker, poured two cups, and handed one to Barty. "I have things laid out in a conference room for you, along with what we think is going on. I figured you could look at it and give us some insight into where we went wrong."

"Would it also be possible to visit each of the shooter locations?" Barty's mind spun quickly, trying to run through what he already knew and where the holes were. That was the easy part, because there were many of those at the moment.

"Of course," Jim said. "I can take you there later this morning or this afternoon."

Barty followed Jim to the conference room and took a seat. He looked through the pictures of the various crime scenes and shooter locations and maps of the various scenes on the board, as well as witness statements. He read fast, but it still took him nearly three hours to review and digest all the information.

"You were very thorough, and your killer is smarter than I originally thought."

"How so?" Jim said as he set another cup of coffee on the table for him.

Barty looked up from his handwritten notes and smiled. "Thank you."

"Anytime." Jim pulled out the chair next to his and sat, watching him intently. "So what insights do you have?" He sipped from his paper cup.

"Well, look here." Barty grabbed one of the pictures. "This roof is composite with an aggregate overlay. You found the bullet calling card here, but there are no footsteps at all and nothing is disturbed. So he either scaled the building somehow or wiped out his tracks...." Barty paused.

"That's what we figured."

"There's a third option. The bullet was there all along." Barty thought out loud. "If I were to plan something like this and I wanted to get even with a town or send some kind of message this way, I'd have scouted out my locations. I'd know them forward and backward… in advance."

"Isn't there the chance they'd be discovered?"

"Why? Anyone who did would simply think them odd. It's only when there's a shooting that they'd make any sense at all. So if I were him—and this is a far-reaching and far-thinking man, a chess player." Barty looked up again. "Yes. He loves chess, or did. And he's thinking eight, maybe ten moves ahead."

"Okay." Jim was taking notes, and Barty returned to the photographs.

"I need to see this location, right now." He stood, waiting for Jim impatiently. "It's supposed to rain in a few hours, and if it does, what I need to see will be gone."

"All right. I'll drive. Let's go." Jim left the conference room, grabbing a camera along the way, led them out to a car, and then drove the few blocks to where the shooting took place.

Barty got out, looking around.

"What are you doing?"

"Looking for the way up," Barty said, checking all the sides of the building.

"There's a stairway to the roof inside." Jim opened the back door, and they went up. "It wasn't locked."

"Nothing like making things easy for us," Barty said, and Jim followed Barty up to the top and then through the door to the roof. "Can I look around?"

"Yes. We found the casing over there."

Barty shook his head. "Where was the victim shot?"

Jim showed him, and Barty nodded, keeping an eye on that spot as he moved around the roof. "Look at this," he said a few minutes later when he spotted three indentations in the aggregate. "Here is where he took the shot. The rifle was on a tripod that left these indentations. My guess is that the casing was planted days before, as soon as this location was chosen. Then, when you came up here, you and your men saw the casing and most likely gave this part of the roof a more cursory look."

21

"But they should have photographed the entire roof, not just the area in question."

Barty shrugged. "Taking a picture of something is fine, but you weren't looking at them because you weren't expecting anything." He stood back up and let Jim do his thing, including taking close-up pictures.

"How did you know?" Jim asked.

"His brilliance." Ideas were still churning in his head. His grandmother had told him that he had a brain like a computer and that sometimes he had to let it do its work. He should never feel pressured to give an answer he wasn't ready for. "He's using misdirection to his advantage." Barty watched as Jim went through a number of emotions in front of him. Academically he knew what they meant, but it was the anger associated with embarrassment that Barty was able to understand most readily.

"Should we go to the other locations?"

"Yes, please." There were theories rolling around that he wanted confirmation of before he vocalized them. They headed back to the stairs. "Why did you become a police officer?" Barty asked as they descended. He had always wanted to know why things happened and why people did the things they did. He never innately understood other people. He knew his childhood was unique and strange—the kids at school had made that plain enough to him—and being a psychologist, he was always asking why. That was the primary question they asked when it came to why people commit violence against each other.

"That's a change in subject," Jim said.

"Not really. We're investigating a crime. It's a natural question." Barty continued down the stairs, waiting for Jim's answer.

"I wanted to help people." Jim stopped and turned to him. and Barty blinked and tried to mimic his look as he waited. "That's the bullshit answer." He turned away, and they continued back to the ground. "I think I picked it at first because it would piss my family off something awful. They had a million expectations for me. My brother is a pediatric oncologist, and my younger sister, who's brilliant and finished high school at the same time I did, is a leading economist at Templeton. I wanted to go my own way."

22

"You thought you couldn't compete, so you didn't," Barty said matter-of-factly. "It's typical of middle children. You need to carve out a place of your own. But you could have done that in a lot of ways—why law enforcement?" People usually closed off to him at about this point, and Barty had been told numerous times that he needed to learn when to back away. But once his curiosity was raised, it was hard for him to turn it off. Besides, there was something about this man, this mind, that intrigued him, and he wasn't sure why.

"Are you a middle child?" Jim asked, and Barty stared back as they stood at the base of the stairwell.

"Yes. But I was like your sister. I graduated from high school ahead of my older sister. I think she was happy to have me gone from the school for her senior year." He rarely had people ask questions of him or about him. It felt like Jim had gotten the better of him somehow. He knew give-and-take was important in any relationship, but he rarely shared things about himself. To him, it was like giving away something that could be used against him. "Again, why law enforcement?"

"I think I always wanted to be a cop. I used to watch them on television, and they were always doing these heroic and interesting things. I was good with guns, and I enjoy unraveling puzzles. It seemed like a good fit, and when I went to the academy, I found out I was right." Jim pushed open the door, and they went back to the street. "I need to remind this owner to get a panic alarm on this door so it can be closed to the outside."

That made sense to Barty, and he waited while Jim made his call. He seemed satisfied with the answer he received, and they continued on. Jim drove them a block down the street to the next location. But any indications that might have remained at one time were gone. Still, Barty got a good view of the scene and played it out in his mind. He saw a shadowy shooter, away from the edge of the roof, lining up his shot, taking it, and then leaving within seconds.

"Is there a way for you to match a bullet you take from a body with the exact shell it came from?" Barty asked, his eyes still closed as he watched the shooter go through his motions in his mind.

"I don't know. There could be. I need to ask. Why?"

"Okay. The shooter will scout out locations, and he doesn't want to leave any indication of himself. Except he does no matter what, and he knows that. So he misdirects you, and he does that by placing the casing at the scene. But what if it isn't the casing he just used? What if it was placed there when he scouted it? There would be no rush—no one would be looking for him because there hasn't been a shooting. He'd also have tested his access and egress."

"So he'd carry a shell casing with him and place it when he scouted?" Jim said, and Barty nodded.

"Maybe the shell casing from the shot he took yesterday will be the one he places at his next location," Barty offered. "Maybe it's already there now."

"Do we need to search for it?" Jim said, and Barty gently touched his arm.

"No. We need to find a way of looking for it without him knowing we're looking for it." Barty's head was ringing. He knew he was on the right idea. Everything sang to him, and that only happened when he knew he was right and he'd made some kind of breakthrough. Behavior was often like a puzzle, and he might have solved a piece of this one.

"But if it's there, we need to find it. Then we'll know his next location."

"If you find it and he knows you've found it.... This is chess, remember? He'll be watching the next location somehow. If he's chosen it, then it's something he values, so it's probably watched and looked after somehow. No, we have to play his game and not let him know we're playing. So far we've been within his rules, but if we disturb some of his planning, he's going to know we're on to him and he'll change the rules."

"How do you know all this?" Jim asked.

Barty ignored that question as another notion took root. "Did your people check for cameras at the locations?"

"Why?"

"He's going to watch them somehow," Barty said as his thoughts continued. He shook his head slowly as a clearer picture emerged. "They'd already be removed. He'd take them away when he arrived to take his shot. He wouldn't leave any visual evidence of him actually shooting someone that could accidentally be recorded." He adjusted the picture in his mind, and it made perfect sense. The shooter removed the camera, set up his equipment, took his shot, policed his brass, and left, redirecting them to a different part of the roof. "Can we look at the others?" Barty asked, and Jim took him to the other locations. They reinforced what Barty thought, but unfortunately didn't provide him with any other insight, so they went back to the station.

Jim was on the phone most of the time, presumably with the lab to see if they could help confirm any of Barty's information. He was pretty pleased that he'd been able to help like that. It didn't always work that way. Getting into the head of another person was never easy, and sometimes it wasn't possible. There had to be a connection, something that allowed the researcher special insight into the subject in order for that to happen. Barty had heard of a researcher who suffered from bipolar disorder, and he was able to gain incredible insight into others with the same affliction and wrote some brilliant papers on the subject.

"Do you want to look over the documentation again to see if anything else comes to mind?" Jim asked, but Barty shook his head.

"There's nothing in there I haven't seen. I already have it all, unless there's something new."

"I take it you have a great memory," Jim said.

"I never forget anything. Good and bad—it's all inside waiting for me."

"And I bet sometimes when you're at low energy, the containers around the bad become weak, and then…."

Barty nodded. "You understand."

"Some of the things I've seen, I wish I could throw the memories away, wipe them clean so I'd never see those images again or have my entire outlook colored by them." Jim sat in one of the chairs, and Barty took the one next to him. "But I can't."

"No. They're always there. The pain of losing the people closest to you." He wasn't sure why he'd said that. Barty rarely shared pieces of his personal life with others. "Of course, there are also the good things that don't go away. I remember winning an award when I was in the second grade. I was very happy, and Nana was there to see me get it." Of course, there was a reason Nana was there instead of his mom and dad, but he kept the door firmly closed on those memories, at least for now.

"Yeah. I have a good memory too, but I doubt it's as sharp as yours." Jim stood. "Wait here a minute." He left the room and returned with another man. "This is Captain Westin. Barty Halloran. We reviewed the various shooter locations, and he has some real potential insight."

They shook hands, with Barty nearly wincing at the strength in the captain's grip. He wasn't as large as Jim but had an intensity that seemed to vibrate off him.

"He thinks the casing could have been planted in advance when he scouted the locations," Jim said.

"So we need to search rooftops?"

"Yes and no. We need to see if there are any cameras. Doing a personal roof-to-roof search will tip him off."

"It isn't like we have cameras in the sky overhead," Captain Westin said, and Barty rolled his eyes.

"Get creative. There have to be ways that rooftops can be viewed. They do it all the time on the news. Helicopters or something. Get high-resolution cameras, take pictures of the town, and then analyze the rooftop images for casings. They take detailed pictures from space."

"I don't think we have access to that technology, but we can look into it." Captain Westin left red-faced, nostrils flaring, and Jim's gaze followed him until he disappeared.

"Man, he's pissed. The captain isn't used to being outsmarted like that."

"Then how can he be the best at his job if his decisions aren't validated? It's only through questioning that our decisions and judgments can prove that they can stand on their own in the light of day. If questioning bothers him, then he mustn't have sound judgments and is afraid of their exposure."

Barty began going through the crime scene pictures one more time, specifically looking for things that he hadn't seen when they visited the crime scenes. Normally he'd rely on his memory, but this was too important. Now that he knew what to look for, he found indications at almost every one of the actual shots being taken from a different location than originally thought. He was on the right track. But Barty knew this was just the surface and the real heart of this matter was going to be ugly.

HE SET up his laptop and spent the rest of the day working through what he'd read and seen to develop a profile of the killer, but there was so much information he was missing that what he came up with was only in general terms, and that frustrated him. He liked his answers to be solid, but what he kept coming back to was nebulous and could apply to millions of people. Jim played the message that had been left for them, and it reinforced Barty's profile but didn't fill in any of the blanks.

Jim had pretty much left him to his own devices for the afternoon, and that was precisely how he liked to work. But Barty found himself checking for Jim every half hour or so. He kept wondering about him, and not in an academic way. First thing, Jim had actually answered Barty's questions honestly, which told him he was a pretty self-aware kind of man. Barty had also divulged things about himself. Academically he knew that could be the start of a friendship, and he liked that notion. He didn't have many real friends. He'd never been good at making them. Mostly he had acquaintances and contacts.

Something else niggled at the back of Barty's mind, but he didn't understand what it was in the least.

"Have you come up with anything?" Jim asked, placing a cup of coffee next to him.

Barty smiled. It was nice that Jim thought of him when he got a coffee for himself. He lifted his gaze from his laptop and caught Jim's smile. It was nice, warm, and genuine. Barty had made a study of smiles as part of his work. People smiled for different reasons—for example, to cover up embarrassment or discomfort. Sometimes a smile could be menacing and chilling. Jim's smile was nothing like those. It was like he was happy to see him. A flutter in his belly that had been simmering all day flared into a flight of butterflies, and Barty wondered if he might have eaten something that didn't agree with him, but there was a pleasant feeling, like an aftertaste.

"I have a basic profile," Barty said, and Jim leaned closer. "It's definitely a man, in my opinion, and he's smart, supersmart." Barty paused before he got into what he wanted to say. "This is all opinion at this point. A theory that we need to prove or change as we get more evidence."

"Like, *you* smart?"

Barty colored. His intelligence was a source of pride for him, but he'd learned that it intimidated other people. "You can be as smart as you like, but don't make others feel dumb," Nana had told him.

"Maybe. But in a different way. He's smart, and at the same time, ruthless and without empathy. He doesn't care what his actions do to others. His entire emphasis is on himself and the effect others have on him." Barty turned away from his computer screen. "He's the kind of subject that people in my profession would love to be able to study. He's aware of his strengths and very good at minimizing his weaknesses. However, the exception is his ego. I think that's what's driven him to this extreme."

"How so?" Jim asked.

"To boil things down, let's say we have two people, both raised in pretty much the same way. But as adults, one turns into a serial killer and the other one studies people who become serial killers." Barty might have been getting a little close to himself, but the example seemed to work in this case. "The two people are like two sides of the same coin. One turns evil, and the other goes on to lead a fairly normal life. One of the things that can help decide which way they go is ego. Let's say that both of them have the potential to climb on rooftops and shoot people. Not everyone is going to do that."

"So the one most likely is the one with a biggest ego?"

"Possibly," Barty said and turned to Jim. "You be the bad guy. You're our serial shooter. You're smart and think you're smarter than everyone else. Therefore, you're the best at everything. So something triggers your superiority. You get passed over for promotion, or flunk a class that you think you should be teaching because the instructor is a complete idiot. Or your girlfriend leaves you for someone else, but of course you're the best lover and best boyfriend in the world, so she should definitely want to be with you. Therefore, something is wrong with the world and you need to change that." When he looked into Jim's eyes, heat built up inside him, and he wondered why the room had suddenly gotten warm. "So you need to change the world and set it back to right where you are better than everyone else. Our shooter is doing just that. There's an event that triggered these episodes, but we don't know where to look for that yet. There is also some escalating event."

"I don't understand."

Barty ran his finger under his collar because it felt a little tight. He lost his train of thought as he momentarily fell into Jim's brown eyes. Barty blinked and got back on track.

"Okay, so we have you as our potential serial shooter. You believe you're better than everyone else. Therefore other people matter less than you do. They're expendable because you're the very best. Something happens that triggers your righteous indignation because things aren't right. Your ego is bruised, but you grind your teeth and continue on, because after all, you are smarter than everyone else and know what's best. But the world doesn't return to where it should be. You are slighted over and over again, and each time the anger and resentment builds and builds. Other inferior people are being promoted over you... whatever it is. Then something happens that sends you over the edge and you have to take action, because the world isn't righting itself and you feel it isn't going to."

"Jesus," Jim said softly.

"The problem is that it often isn't until after the fact that we're able to piece these incidents together and come up with a real cause or answers. Sometimes we never can at all. There are people who would be fantastic research subjects, but they won't talk. Others do nothing but talk, but their information is so skewed and facts hard to corroborate that we get no usable data." Barty sipped his coffee, then set it aside. He was still too warm. "Is there something cold to drink?"

"Sure. Give me a minute." Jim left, and Barty breathed as normally as possible, trying to determine the cause of this reaction. Jim returned with a bottle of water that had condensation on the outside, and Barty opened it and drank half. "How do we use this to try to find him?"

"I'm still working on some things. There are a number of possibilities. A lot of superintelligent people work in academia because many of us don't have superior social skills. Though I'm not saying that's a given, but it might be a place to start. You could try MENSA, but I don't think that's the kind of group our shooter would join. He'd surround himself with smart people, but no one potentially smarter than he is. That way he's always the biggest and best in the room." Barty stopped. "Chess clubs," he added.

"You said that this is a game a couple of times."

"Yes. He thinks many moves ahead, and that's something chess players do. So try looking at the various chess clubs, but only at the very top players. He'd definitely be one of the best…."

"Or he wouldn't be in the club," Jim said, and Barty nodded.

"Exactly. He set this whole thing up as a game, one he was sure to win. Oh, and he isn't above cheating. The rules have little value to him. So he'd think nothing of changing them in the middle of the game, especially one of his own creation."

Jim left the room, and Barty saw him talking to a few other officers. The two men Barty didn't know nodded and then hurried back to their desks.

Jim returned to the conference room. "Apparently the captain pulled a few strings and is lining up a helicopter and working on a camera with enough resolution. I have officers checking chess clubs for a list of members."

"Good. You know… maybe I was wrong. Maybe our shooter joined something like MENSA and then left. You might try former members. It isn't likely that his ego would allow him to stay active, but the entrance score would be validation of how smart he really is."

"Are you a member?"

Barty returned his attention to his computer. "It doesn't matter to me. I know I'm smart enough and that I'm good at what I do. But I don't have the need for a lot of that kind of outside validation." He'd also never thought of himself as a particularly social person, so clubs and memberships had never been the kind of things on his radar screen. "I honestly don't know how much more help I can be to you at this point. I've gotten all the information I can from what you have." And he was starting to get tired. It had been a long day, and he was ready to go home. Although the thought of driving back into the city at this time of day was a pretty frightening prospect.

"Would you be willing to continue working on this with us?"

Barty started the shutdown process on his computer and then turned away from it. "Of course. You can call me when you need something. I have to teach my classes, but I have a light load right now, so I can help." He packed up his things and checked the time. "Is there a place nearby where I can get dinner? I don't really like to drive and it's the height of rush hour right now, so maybe if I eat, some of the worst traffic will be over." He wasn't hopeful, but everyone was hitting the freeways right now and it was going to be a zoo.

"Certainly. There are a few decent places." Jim waited for him and walked him out. "If you like, I can take you to dinner. You've been a big help."

"You don't have to do that," Barty said. He usually ate alone, with only Penelope for company.

"It will be nice." Jim led him outside and down to a small restaurant less than a block from the station. "It isn't fancy."

Barty continually looked around them for any sign of a shooter. There were very few people out, which made sense if you had someone taking shots at people on the street. "Everyone is battened down and nervous," Barty observed.

"Yeah. Not that I can blame them. This whole thing has everyone jittery and bothered. Though if the pattern holds, it could be weeks before there's another incident." Jim didn't open the door right away. "That's the real problem. Just about the point that people start to think that everything has passed and their lives can return to normal, there will be another shooting." He opened the door and let Barty step inside.

The restaurant was nice and well lit, with small flower vases on each table displaying a few blooms. "Please sit wherever you like," the server said, and Jim led them to an out-of-the-way table.

"Is this okay? I thought we could talk," Jim explained, and Barty sat down in the chair across from Jim. "I hate that I can't seem to put an end to this. The next step is to call in the FBI, but police departments are so territorial, and I think we're making progress."

"You were and are. No one is perfect, so we'll catch him. He's already left some clues I don't think he intended to, and the phone call was very telling. I'd expect more of those. They're a cry for attention. Also expect some escalation on his part. He wants his message to get through even though he may say he doesn't."

"Sometimes the waiting is the hardest part."

"True. But we were able to come up with a number of avenues of inquiry that I think are new. They may pan out or they may not, but if one of them does, you'll be closer to an answer." Barty picked up the menu and looked it over.

"See anything you like?" Jim asked and then checked his phone as the server approached.

"Yes. I'd like a glass of water to drink, and I'll have your Cobb salad without tomatoes or olives. And please put the Italian dressing on the side." He handed her the menu, and Jim ordered a burger with a small salad on the side.

"You made me want to be good. Usually I get fries." Jim grinned briefly, and that fluttery feeling from earlier in the day returned.

Barty got warm again, and he was starting to get a little excited. He knew what sex was and that it was a normal part of life. But he'd never actually had any real sex with another person. He also knew he liked boys because he used to think about them in… that way… when he was a teenager. That was something he never talked to his nana about, and Barty was more than glad about that. The thought of talking to her about those urges had been mortifying.

His water arrived, and Barty drank most of the glass before asking for a refill.

"What was it like growing up for you? You said you graduated high school ahead of your older sister. That must have caused some issues for you."

Barty nodded and thought about what he wanted to say. "As a psychologist, I can look back on all that and understand what was going on, but back then it was so confusing. I have an older sister and a younger brother, Mark. Nicole is a beauty consultant in a salon in Erie, Pennsylvania. She wants to own her own place, but I don't think she has what it takes to do that. But, of course, I can never say that to her."

"Because you know it will hurt her feelings?"

Barty did know that in his own way. "Actually she'd yell at me about not supporting her, and then she'd probably rip things off me the next time I saw her. I mean, why wouldn't someone want to fully understand their capabilities? If she isn't able to run a shop of her own and opens one, she'll lose all kinds of money and will be worse off than she is now. Practically it doesn't make sense. But then I also know that it's her dream, and no one likes to have their dreams taken away, so I keep quiet, and she doesn't threaten to castrate me."

"You're so funny," Jim said, and Barty wondered if he was making fun of him. "I like how you look at both sides of things." Ah, he was serious. That was nice, and Jim was smiling again, which started the flutters once more.

"No one thinks I'm humorous," Barty said.

"Then they haven't spent time with you. Most people would go for the quick answer and the castration. You looked at all the answers and came to the same conclusion. What about your brother?"

Barty chuckled nervously. "He scares me. Mark is a biker. He works in a garage that services motorcycles, and has a club that he rides with. I think they're a gang, but he says they're a club and that there is nothing illegal going on. My mother worries about him all the time, but he's old enough to make his own decisions."

"It sounds like he's the rebel in your family."

"He definitely is. Though his older brother, who went to college and got his PhD at twenty-three, is the weird one to him. Mark thinks he's normal, and from what I know, of the two of us, he probably is. He apparently has a girlfriend who is very nice, according to my mom, and Mom thinks she'll be a good influence."

"Do you see your mom and dad often?" Jim asked, but Barty shook his head.

33

"They're in Erie and I live here. They have the other two, and...." The server refilled his water and left the table. "I was too much for them. At least that's what Nana used to say. My mom couldn't handle me, so I was sent to live with her mother here in Philadelphia. She and my dad could raise the other two, but there were no resources for me there, and so I was sent to Nana and she raised me. I got the attention I needed, and she was able to get me into the best schools. Nana also helped me try to understand other people and pushed me to go into psychology. She said it would help me understand people in a way that didn't come naturally to me."

"I looked you up on the web this afternoon. It's amazing the things you've accomplished and all the awards you've won."

"They're nice, but not the end-all. Mostly I like the work, and Nana was right. I don't understand most people, and sometimes I don't understand myself, but my research allows me to get the answers I need and allows me to help other people at the same time."

The server placed his salad in front of him, and Barty checked that it was right before thanking her softly.

"What was your grandmother like?" Jim took a bite of his burger and set it back down on the plate.

"She was fun and did a lot of things with me. We went to concerts and things like that. Nana lived in a small house near a park, which I visited a lot to watch the other kids play." Barty took a bite of his salad. "She died when I was seventeen and at college."

"That must have been very hard for you. I knew my grandparents, but I never lived with them like that. My grandpa was very special to me. I think he was the one who might have figured out that I was different from the other kids, though we never really talked about it."

Barty put a few of the pieces together and nodded slowly. He understood that feeling well. Not only was he a gay kid, but he was supersmart, so the kids had pretty much stayed away.

"I never talked about things like that with Nana either. I don't think I could have, though I talked with her about other things. At first I thought it made me a bad person, and then, of course, I learned in school that it was just part of the person I was, but I never told her. I've thought about why and never came up with a reason."

"Maybe you just weren't ready," Jim offered. It was a simple answer and probably the best.

"Sometimes we want grand explanations for things, when the easiest and most logical is the best."

"I wasn't ready to tell Grandpa. He probably would have listened and supported me all the way, but I wasn't ready to open up." Jim watched him from across the table. "You don't have to answer if you don't want, but you said your parents couldn't handle you. What did that mean? Did you act out?"

Barty wasn't sure he wanted to answer that question. "Well, no. My parents learned I was smart and wanted to give me everything, so they enrolled me in violin lessons, piano lessons, many things. I could read before I was four, so I was given all kinds of books and things like that. My brother and sister had normal toys, and I was given instruments, music, books.... The thing was, I wasn't allowed to just spend time and play. As soon as they figured out I was special, then I had to be special as far as they were concerned."

"I don't understand. Why is that bad?" Jim watched him closely, and Barty felt self-conscious. Whenever he talked about himself like this, he always felt a little like he was on display. "Isn't wanting a gifted child to be the best they can and have all the advantages so they can make the most of themselves a good thing?"

"It is. But Mom and Dad went overboard. There is too much of a good thing. See, I didn't play with other children much growing up because I was always doing things they couldn't." Barty sat back. "We learn empathy and how to deal with other people through play. First we play alone, then we progress to playing side by side with other kids, and finally we play in groups. That's the natural progression of things. I never got to do any of it, except some alone play when I wasn't at lessons, and mostly it was with my books and things. I didn't understand how to be with other kids, so I never even got the basics. When I went to school for the first time, I remember standing in one of the corners just watching the other kids. They would talk to each other and play together, and I didn't know what to do. I was terrified and didn't understand. There was a teacher's aide, I think, a black woman, who came over to me and asked me if I wanted to play with the blocks. I was four years old and didn't know what to do with them. I clearly remember sitting down in front of them, staring at the pile, completely lost."

"My God," Jim said.

"Exactly. Eventually I learned to make towers and stuff, but there was never any joy in it, just stress and things I was supposed to remember. After a few years, Mom and Dad didn't know what to do, and Nana came and took me to live with her. I still didn't understand other kids, but she tried to help me." Barty had talked enough. He always felt like a freak of sorts. He was smart, and that set him apart from other people, but the whole play thing sort of bothered him. He remembered learning in class about how children developed and realizing how his own childhood was so stilted. Then he learned the consequences of that kind of deprivation, and it chilled him to the bone. He didn't want to talk about that anymore. Barty turned his attention back to his salad. He ate rather quickly because if his mouth was full, then he couldn't be expected to speak.

"I grew up just the opposite of you, I guess you could say. We had money, so I had the best of everything—a pony, toys, a pool, lessons, sports. My sister still rides and is very good. Both my brother and sister are smart. I told you what they did. I'm just an average guy. My parents are the kings and queens of denial. They're very much about society and how things look to other people. Being gay isn't on their list of things they want their son to be."

Barty set down his fork. "Don't they know that sexual orientation is a biological thing that is determined at birth? It's part of who you are, just like the color of your eyes. We don't get to choose that, no matter how much some of us may want to."

Jim grinned. Barty liked how Jim looked when he did that. Jim was a big guy with rangy hair that seemed to go everywhere. But he had a handsome face with a slightly swoopy nose and intense brown eyes. His hair, not that Barty usually noticed such things, was a little long and bedheady. Sort of like Barty's except Jim's might have been intentional; Barty's bedhead was because he forgot to do anything with his hair most of the time. Jim was gorgeous, at least Barty thought so, and he looked strong, with wide shoulders. He bet Jim worked out quite a bit.

"I think I'd pay money to hear you tell my mother that," Jim said with a chuckle.

"Facts are facts, and disputing them is only another form of denial and self-delusion." Barty continued eating.

"I'd pay for you to say that too." Jim returned to his dinner and began laughing to himself. "This Sunday my sister is having a garden party to celebrate her promotion to department head. It would be awesome if you came."

"Why would you want me there?" Barty asked. "I always do something to stand out in a bad way. The last party I went to was in college, and I ended up telling the president of the university that he needed to rethink his theories on student behavior and the rules he was making because, rather than changing the way the students who smoked behaved, they were simply finding ways around his rules. In the end the students continued doing exactly what they wanted in the first place and pissed off everyone who had to walk through the walls of smoke to get where they were going. I went on to say that if they thought things through more thoroughly, they might avoid such untenable decisions in the future."

"Good God," Jim said. "Do you always state what's on your mind like that?"

"No. I try to do what's socially acceptable, but it doesn't work out because I don't know all the rules. I end up embarrassing people so I just avoid situations like that."

"What about friends? Don't you get together with them?"

"I don't have those kind of friends," Barty said, and to his shock, Jim reached across the table and took his hand. It tingled where Jim touched him, and his first instinct was to pull away, but then he realized he liked it when Jim touched him. His hand was warm and firm, slightly rough, and strong.

"Well, you do now. I think you're an interesting guy and I like you." He squeezed his hand once and then released it. "And my sister always expects that invitees to her parties will bring a guest, so I'd like you to come. And I want you to be yourself and talk to anyone you like."

"Is this a joke?"

"No. It's most definitely not. You said you didn't know how to act around others, so the only way to learn is to be around others. So come to the party with me. If I know my sister, there will be enough incredible food to make the day worthwhile on that stand alone." Jim returned to his dinner. As he finished the burger, his phone dinged. "I have to get back. There's been another shooting."

Barty jumped to his feet and was ready to go in seconds. "What about the check?"

Their server rushed over. "Is something wrong?"

"Yes. Detective Crawford. I have to go. Tell Janine that I'll be in to pay the bill as soon as I can. She'll understand." Jim was already heading toward the door, and Barty ran behind him, heart pounding at the chance to see one of the crime scenes up close and personal. Outside, sirens sounded, and Jim raced toward them as fast as his feet would carry him. Barty stretched his long legs and did his best to keep up as the wails got louder and louder.

# CHAPTER 3

ONE GOOD thing about New Cynwood was that nothing was ever too far away. "Where are we going?"

"West Laurel Hill Cemetery, by the sound of it. They weren't specific in their message so I'm following the sirens at this point." Jim grabbed his phone when it rang. "Yeah?"

"The shooting is at the edge of the cemetery," the dispatcher said.

"I'm already on my way on foot. Have someone pick us up." He gave their location, and within seconds a car turned on the street and sped toward them. Jim flagged them down, and they got inside. "Let's go."

"Do you really think it's another shooting?" Barty asked.

"If it is, then he's escalating. Last time it was over ten days. So I don't know, but we can't take the chance," Jim said as they sped toward the scene. When they arrived, Jim jumped out of the car and raced to where the ambulance and other cars were congregated. "What do we have?"

"Who is that?" one of the officers asked, looking at Barty, who took a step back.

"He's with me, now answer my question." He wasn't in the mood for deflection.

"Looks like some kids decided that the cemetery was a good place for a gun fight." The victim lay on the ground, clutching his arm, while ambulance personnel worked to try to get the bleeding under control. "He's the shooter."

"It was self-defense," said a kid in clothes expensive enough to cost a month of Jim's salary. "He challenged me, and I had to defend my honor."

"Take him in and book him. Self-defense in a situation you willingly put yourself in? I don't think so." Jim took a deep breath and then leaned

39

down to the young man on the ground. He turned away to roll his eyes, then turned back. "What do you have to say for yourself?"

"I didn't think the gun was loaded." The kid gritted his teeth in pain, and the EMT didn't look a bit sorry about it. Not for a second.

Jim turned the case over to the sergeant in charge and stepped away. They were more than capable of handling this mess, and he didn't need to be involved. "I'll get a ride back to the station in a few minutes once the activity here dies down."

"Does stuff like this happen often?" Barty asked.

"This is a new one. Maybe they thought the cemetery was Boston Common." He meant it as a joke, but Barty was obviously interested in the young man.

"Do you think I can talk to them? I'd really like to know what they were thinking when they came up with a scheme like this." He was clearly fascinated.

"They'll lawyer up tight as soon as we get them back to the station. The lawyers aren't going to let you talk to either of them in case you're working with us. But you're welcome to ask. They aren't going to see a judge tonight, so the one will be in the hospital and his friend will be in jail. New Cynwood isn't a town per se. We're part of Lower Merion Township. We have a police station here because the residents demand it, but these two will have to go to the county courthouse to be arraigned, so he'll be processed there and get to be a guest of the county."

"Oh."

"Like I said, we can ask and see if they'll talk to you." That made Barty happier, and Jim wondered why that was suddenly important to him. Yeah, he'd said that he wanted to be Barty's friend, but there was something more. Granted, he had no intention of going further than friendship, but still, his need to please Barty was a little baffling.

"So this doesn't have anything to do with the other shootings?"

"It doesn't seem to." Jim was relieved. They needed some time to try to figure out how they were going to catch this shooter. The possible courses of action they were putting into place might yield results, but then again, they might not. "Here's our ride," Jim explained when Tag, one of the officers, caught his attention, lifting the bags they'd left in the other car. They left the scene to the others and took the ride back to the station. "How is the freeway, Tag?" Jim asked as they rode. He hadn't wanted Barty sitting in the backseat alone. It could be intimidating knowing that was where suspects were transported.

"The Surekill is backed up for miles. There's an accident just outside of downtown that has traffic snarled in both directions, and then there's one just a mile up going north. So everything is tied in knots and will be for hours." The Schuylkill was notorious for accidents and had been nicknamed the Surekill because of the number of fatalities.

Barty groaned softly.

"Don't worry," Jim said.

"I hate that road," Barty said. "It always makes me nervous and jittery." His hand was shaking just talking about it.

"How do you get to work?" Tag asked from the front seat in a smooth, rich voice.

"Mostly I bicycle when I can. I hate driving but do it when I must." Barty's right leg bounced up and down with more energy as the seconds ticked by. "I came in so early this morning to try to avoid the traffic, but I knew I'd have to drive home in it." He held his bag in front of him with his arms clasped around it like a shield.

"Really?" Tag asked like he'd never heard of such a thing before. Thankfully they reached the station a few minutes later, and Jim got out, motioning Barty inside. He didn't lower his bag.

"It's okay about the driving thing. I've taken courses in high-speed chases and ultimate driver control, and I hate the Surekill with a passion." He checked at the desk and found the backup wasn't going anywhere. Both accidents involved fatalities, so the freeway was going to be jammed well into the night.

"I'll find an alternate way home," Barty said.

"I have an hour or so of work, and then you can stay with me and go home tomorrow if you need to."

The surprise on Barty's face was priceless. "But I don't have anything with me, and Penelope is at home alone." He sounded really stressed.

"Who's Penelope?"

"My cat. I always leave her extra food and water, but…." The way he worried about the cat was most definitely endearing. "I don't like her to be alone."

"All right. Let me get my work done and you can come to the house for a few hours. By then the accidents should be cleared and traffic can move once again."

This was the strangest day in his entire career. Jim walked to the conference room and let Barty use it while he went to his desk to see if any additional information had come in.

After reviewing his e-mail, Jim made his way back to the conference room. "Barty, there was water inside two of the shell casings." He'd printed the report and showed it to Barty. "That means that those casings had to have been up there long enough for it to have rained or for water to condense into them. So your theory holds water, so to speak." He handed him the report and grinned. At least they were making progress on something.

"So…."

"That means the casings are being placed in advance, so if we can locate them, then maybe we can catch this guy in the act before he kills again."

Jim phoned the captain to tell him what they'd confirmed, and Captain Westin said that he'd contacted some buddies who were going to make a pass over the area in a helicopter to take aerial photographs. He wasn't sure how much that would help or if they could get enough detail, but it was worth a try, and he was willing to try just about anything at this point.

"My next step is the military. I have contacts, and I'll see if we can get satellite images, but looking for a single shell on the roof of a building is going to be like finding a needle in a mile-high haystack."

"I agree," Jim said, but he wasn't sure what other options there were. It wasn't like they could invisibly watch every rooftop in the area. There had to be something they could do, but no ideas were coming. He hung up. "I think I'm ready to go. I got an update, and the officers are running down chess clubs and MENSA. They expect to have something tomorrow, so we can leave for the night."

Barty closed his laptop and packed up. Jim made sure all of the case files were organized and gathered them to be filed. Then he locked the conference room behind them and led Barty out. Jim went to his car and waited for Barty, then drove slowly home and pulled into the drive with Barty right behind him.

"Is this where you live?"

"It was my grandfather's," Jim said, heading up the walk and inside, deactivating the alarm at the front door. He didn't normally come in this way, but he figured he could give Barty the full effect of the house, with the grand hall, staircase, and huge chandelier that crowned the space. "He left it to me when he died. Grandma passed a decade earlier, and he lived here alone. Come on in. We'll go to the family room—it's much more comfortable and less stuffy."

Jim motioned him through and turned on lights as they went. In the family room, he handed Barty the television remote and got some water from the refrigerator, along with some fruit and crackers to make up for their interrupted dinner.

"Make yourself comfortable. The furniture is fine to put your feet up on." Jim sighed as he sat. "I bought this stuff to be lived on, unlike the rest of the house, which is more museum than home."

"Your family has a lot of money," Barty said, looking around with an open mouth. Even this room was impressive, with high ceilings, detailed moldings, tons of woodwork, and floors that shone.

"Yes. My grandpa inherited money and had the golden touch. He made it by the ton and passed it on to my dad and us three kids. But when he died, he specifically left me the house because he hoped I'd take care of it and pass it on. It was designed by a famous architect in the twenties, and Grandpa loved the place, especially since he and Grandma collected most of the things that are inside." He closed his eyes and tried to relax. This case had him constantly wound up. "Watch whatever you'd like."

Barty shrugged. "I don't watch much television. So I really don't know what's on."

Jim flipped through the channels until he found a *Big Bang Theory* rerun. "Have you seen this?"

Barty shrugged.

"You kind of remind me of Sheldon, except he's way more annoying." He sat back, and Barty watched the show, laughing at the antics.

"I'm not like him at all," he said once the show was over. "He's really annoying, and I try not to be. Though I can be a little inflexible, I suppose, but that guy is a pain in the ass."

"The actor who plays Sheldon is gay." He figured it might be smart to change the subject.

Barty didn't react to that. "Is he your kind of man?" He turned while Jim was still swallowing his teeth. He hadn't been expecting that kind of question.

"My ex is a professor. Philosophy at Stanford, and my boyfriend before that was a professor. Neither of them lasted." Jim was treading on thin ice, and he hoped Barty would let it go. But that was too much to wish for.

"So you like professors." Barty was grinning like some cat who ate the canary.

"I suppose I have a type. Don't we all, Professor?" Jim waggled his eyebrows.

"I'm not familiar personally with any research on the subject. But then there is a lot out there, and everyone can't be familiar with all of it. So I guess I could say that I don't really know." Jim shook his head, and after about five seconds, Barty slapped his hand over his mouth. "You were teasing me."

"Yes."

"I am like that character," Barty gasped. "That's awful."

"No. You just remind me of him a little. You aren't annoying. Oh, and Sheldon doesn't drive, so there's one thing you have on him. You are willing to drive."

"Gee, thanks," Barty said. "So because the question made you so uncomfortable and psychologists love uncomfortable questions, is this professor thing you have going on your only attractor, or are there others?"

"You mean what's my ideal guy?" Jim leaned forward. "You know, if you want to play this game, then you have to be prepared to answer the questions too, and I'm a cop. We specialize in questions that people don't want to answer."

Barty shifted slightly in the chair.

"I seem to have a thing for professor types, especially tall, skinny guys, kind of geeky, with glasses. Particularly glasses. I think they're hot, and there are things I like to do with the glasses when we're in bed." Jim figured he might as well have some fun. If Barty wanted to go there, he was sure as hell going to make the journey as fascinating as possible.

Barty swallowed, and Jim saw a crack in his composure. "Are those the only kind of guys you like?"

"No. I suppose there are others. I mean, a handsome man is a handsome man, if you know what I mean. But I like men who are smart and fun to be around. I guess that once the sex wears off, I like there to be someone to talk to." He was quickly getting much deeper into this conversation than he intended to. This was supposed to be a game, and now he was spilling his guts to Barty about things he didn't talk to anyone about. Barty was obviously very good at getting people to talk to him. "So what's your type?" Jim asked, the whole goose-and-gander thing coming into play.

Barty seemed lost. "I don't know."

Suddenly the conversation had shifted from playful to much too serious, and Jim hadn't really realized it until he'd opened his mouth to say something really stupid and then stopped himself. Teasing Barty at a moment like this wasn't a good idea.

"Are you saying what I think you're saying?" He swallowed. "Barty, you're a handsome man and you have a lot to offer."

"Thank you, I guess, but no one has seemed interested."

Jim got up and went back to the refrigerator. He grabbed a couple of beers and returned, handing one to Barty. "If we're going to have this kind of conversation, we deserve a beer." He popped his open and drank half of it to give Barty a chance to figure out what to say. Now Jim was warm and tugging at his collar. Part of it was the fact that Barty had just gone up a few steps on his attractive scale, and he was nervous that he might say the wrong thing.

"I don't really drink."

"That isn't the point," Jim said as he sat back in his chair, which felt much less comfortable than it had. "You've never been with anyone?" he asked, and Barty shook his head. "Not in any way?"

Another shake of the head, and Barty opened the beer and took a tentative sip before setting it aside.

"You know that's okay."

"Sure it is. I mean, I know who and what I am. I'm a geeky, kind of weird guy who teaches people about the pathology of rapists and murderers. That isn't the kind of guy people line up to date." Barty put his hand in the air and waved his hand like a kid in first grade. "Yeah, please pick me, I want to sleep with the guy who studies serial killers because he was afraid that he might turn into one." He was trying to be funny, only it wasn't.

"What do you mean, you're afraid you might turn into one?" Jim asked, his police officer senses on high alert.

"There are some commonalities between the people I study and myself. Remember how I told you I was raised with everything structured and organized, without time for play like the other kids, because I was *special*? That lack of play leads to a lack of empathy. I've had to learn to understand how other people feel. It's not instinctual, and I get it wrong a lot of the time. That's a trait many of the subjects I study exhibit. Do you remember the man who shot people from the clock tower at the University of Texas? It was people like me trying to figure out why he did what he did that started this line of research, and when I first encountered it, my own picture stared me in the face, so to speak. I nearly freaked."

"But you haven't done anything like that, have you?"

"Of course not!" Barty answered, jumping to his feet.

"Then why worry about it?" Jim asked. "We don't punish people for their potential to do things, only for their actions."

"But I could. It's inside me." Barty patted his chest.

Jim didn't want to believe it. "I'm a cop, right? And some cops take bribes and shift to the dark side of the law. Does that mean that I could do that? That I have the potential? Probably. Have I and will I? No. Because I choose not to. I believe we all have free will and make our own decisions. You may have the potential to shoot people from a bell tower, but that doesn't mean you will. Our killer may have the same potential, but he chose to act on it. Do you really believe that he doesn't know what he's doing?"

"No. You're right. He's choosing to do this."

"And under the same circumstances, what would you choose?" Jim asked and became worried when Barty didn't answer right away.

"I don't know, because I haven't been presented with those circumstances." Barty truly seemed baffled.

"I think you do. See, from what you've said, it's likely our shooter didn't have your nana."

Barty jumped forward. "Of course. Nana is like my conscience. Of course. How could I have missed that? She's the voice in my head that helps me understand the consequences of my actions and their effect on others." He grinned. "That's why we never see ourselves as research subjects. We never see ourselves as clearly as we think we do." He sat back down. "But that doesn't really change anything. The potential is still inside. With the right triggers and pushing, I could be the shooter."

Jim finished his beer and set the empty bottle on the table. Their conversation had taken a turn he hadn't expected at all. From teasing each other about who they like to talking about compulsions that lead to shooting sprees. Time spent with Barty wasn't dull, that's for sure.

"I can't argue with you because I don't have the facts to back me up. All I know is what I believe." And Jim wanted to think that Barty wasn't capable of shooting anyone. "I think there's a lot more to who we are and how we behave than just how our parents treat us and whether we have a chance to play or not." He got up, grabbed his phone, and pulled up a traffic application. He could call in to the station, but it was easier if he didn't have to disturb them. "It looks like the freeway is moving again."

"Thank you for the beer and for the dinner," Barty said. "I'll do some more research on what we've found to see if I have any more ideas that we can apply."

Jim walked Barty back through the house and out to his car. "Drive safely, and I'll be in touch when we have something new." He hoped to hell it wasn't another shooting. Jim waited as Barty got into his car and then pulled out of the drive and away from the house. He didn't go inside right away, watching after Barty and wondering what the hell had just happened.

Barty was someone special, incredibly interesting, and as much as he hated to admit it, attractive as all hell. In many ways Barty pushed his buttons, but he'd told himself more than once that he wasn't going down that path again. The crap with Garrett was more than enough heartbreak to last one lifetime, and his fascination with geeky guys with glasses had already led him astray more than once. He'd told Barty that he believed people made their own choices, and he was going to choose to date a different kind of guy, and that was all there was to it. On top of that, he'd already seen more of humanity's worst than any man had a right to. So why in the hell would he open himself up again? It was easier to just live his life and do his job.

With that decided, he closed his front door, shutting the outside world away for a little while and closing the book on any thoughts he might have had for Barty Halloran. They were going to work together, that was all, and the incredibly hot, innocent, and thought-provoking man in the hottest, geekiest set of glasses on God's green earth was going to remain only a colleague and nothing more.

Jim's resolution was sound, and he was determined. He checked the clock and actually thought about going out for the evening to some place where he could have a little fun and maybe get some action. All these thoughts about Barty had to be frustration building around the fact that he hadn't gotten laid in so very long. There were plenty of clubs where he could find someone interesting for a few hours. When Jim turned around, he bumped his briefcase and it fell on its side, scattering papers on the floor.

"Right," Jim said to himself as he gathered them up. He had work to do and reports and evidence to review yet again. His case was the most important one that his community had seen in years, and he was going to catch this guy if it was the last thing he did. Clubs and boyfriends, all kinds, geeky or not, were going to have to wait until this thing was over and their shooter was behind bars.

Jim activated the alarm and turned off the lights except in the family room, where he spread out his papers and got to work. There was a solution in here somewhere, and he needed to figure out what it was.

After working for hours, Jim sat back in his chair, letting his eyes drift closed. He saw Barty almost immediately, as big as life, smiling like he had over dinner, only now it was from behind a rifle looking down from a rooftop. Jim woke with a start, half expecting to see a pair of crosshairs superimposed over him. But everything was fine. Still, he was out of sorts and the chill didn't dissipate. Jim needed to get some rest and try to let his mind clear. He'd been cramming everything into it, and talking to Barty had mixed everything up in his head.

# CHAPTER 4

BARTY DIDN'T sleep at all that night, or the one after. His day had been full, and he'd talked to Jim. They were still running down the leads on the various organizations.

"Is there anything you might be able to tell us so we know what we're looking for?"

"I wish I did," Barty told him. "Other than to look for the best chess player, the club champion. If he's a member, it's going to be because he's the best of the best. Though I'll admit that's a stretch, but it's worth a shot. I'm really curious as to how he could get the equipment needed to make the kind of shots he's making from the roofs without anyone seeing him. I mean, a lot can be said for people not looking for someone, but I think after what's happened, that everyone would be on the lookout."

"Guns and shooting equipment can be very compact," Jim said. "But you're right. We're looking for someone who is very adept at blending into the crowd when he wants to. This isn't someone who leaves anything to chance."

Barty got a flash of inspiration. "I bet he does trial runs. Without the gun, of course, but he has to be there a day or so ahead of time to set the casings. If you haven't, check with the people in the buildings used as shooting nests and see if they remember seeing someone a few days prior to the shooting."

"I have officers on that right now. He has to show up somewhere, and someone will have to have seen him."

Barty had to get to a class, so he'd ended the call and then had to hurry. That call had been yesterday, and he hadn't heard from Jim since. Granted, it was less than a day, but he was anxious about it and thought of calling him. Instead, he called his sister. Sometimes she understood things that he didn't.

"Barty, how's the world of crazy killers?" Nicole said when she answered the phone.

"Interesting. I'm working with the police on a case." He was happy to have been asked to consult. "It's a good one, and I think I'm helping." He wanted to.

"You be careful," Nicole told him. "Don't get in the line of fire or anything. Though if you're a consultant, you probably stay in your office where it's safe."

"I'm pretty much working out of the police station, but I got to visit the crime scenes, and I'm starting to think the way he does and it's scaring me a little. I think the killer is a lot like me."

"How so?" Nicole asked.

"I think he had a different childhood, like I did. It's a little disturbing to see someone that you could become on the other side of the work I'm doing. Like we're two sides of the same coin."

"You know that isn't true because you'd never hurt anyone. Yeah, you're my supersmart brother who looks at everything from a completely different angle, and you always have to know *why*. You're worse than Danielle, and she's three. But hurt someone... I don't think so. Think of it this way: you're worried about something happening. Therefore, it won't. Does that make sense?" She was way smarter than most people gave her credit for, including Barty, and he needed to change that. "Is that all that has you upset? Because you could just back away if you need to."

"No...," he answered quickly. "There are things I don't understand." He was very uncomfortable talking about things like this, but he needed someone, and Nicole was his best resource for more personal, emotional stuff. "The guy I'm working with... I...." He was rarely at a loss for words. "Okay. I get this weird feeling in my belly when I'm around him, and then I'm hot all the time. I was wondering if I was sick, because I felt flushed a few times and—"

Nicole cut him off with laughter. "You like him." It wasn't a question.

"Yes. He's really interesting, and he seemed to talk to me like I'm not just some freak who should have the answers to all his problems."

51

"No. I mean you *like him* like him. Is he good-looking?" Nicole asked. "Give me details."

"You're not helping."

"Sure I am. Now just answer the question," she said firmly.

"He has really nice brown eyes, and his hair looks like he has bedhead all the time, but I think that's because he's always really busy. He's a little shorter than me but with wider shoulders, and I think he's pretty strong."

"Does he have a nice backside?"

"Nicole!"

"Well, does he?" She could be like a terrier with a bone sometimes.

"Yes. I followed him up some stairs and peeked. He's really handsome, but what does that have to do with it?"

"Barty. When was the last time you noticed anything like that about anyone? You never talk about people's hair or their shoulders and stuff. You were always more interested in what's going on in their head—which was pretty freaky at times, let me tell you—than you ever were about the color of someone's eyes. You like this policeman. Does he like you?"

"I think so. Maybe. I don't know."

"Is he gay? Because if not, you don't want to go there."

She sounded like she knew from firsthand experience, and he really wanted to find out how…. He pulled his thoughts back to the current conversation.

"He is. We had dinner the other night."

"Was it a date?"

"No. I think he was saying thank you because I helped him. Then there was a shooting and we had to go, but it wasn't for the case and they caught the guys. But the freeway was backed up bad, so he asked me back to his house and we talked and I kept feeling weird and anxious. My stomach did these little flips, and I thought it may have been the food, but I didn't know. The house seemed cool enough, but I was hot, and then… things happened and I thought I might have daydreamed about him a little. But then we changed the conversation and we talked about me. Then I went home."

"Did you take a breath?" Nicole teased. She was one of the few people that he knew when she was teasing. Usually because it was a lot of the time, so it was a good bet. "And I stick with what I said before. You like him. There's nothing wrong with that."

"Yes, there is. I don't know what to do about it. What if he doesn't like me that way? Should I ask him, or do I…? This is so complicated. He's a smart guy, and I think I really might like him."

"It sounds like you do. So you can tell him, if you want, and see how he feels. You can work with him and say nothing and hope he says something, but that sucks because all you end up doing is wondering if every little thing is him trying to tell you something. Believe me, those kinds of games are pretty bad. You can also just forget about it, work together, and go home every night and sleep with your cat." Nicole was a dog person, and she'd never liked cats.

"Penelope is a good cat."

"I'm sure she is. But unless you want to live your life with a series of cats for company, you're going to have to take a chance and find someone that you like to spend your life with. Being loved is a good thing."

"I didn't say I was in love with him," Barty explained.

"No. But you're in like with him, and that's a good thing. So if you want my advice, I'd say you should talk to him when you get the chance. Feel him out and see if he acts the same way. Look for signs that he gets warm around you. And watch the way he looks at you. Guys watch you if they're interested. It's part of the whole 'guys are visual' thing. You're good at observing people, so watch him and see what it tells you."

Barty leaned back in his office chair, glad the door was closed. "So what should I do? Talk to him, watch him. This is all so confusing. If this is what I missed from high school by going to college so early, I'm dang glad."

"Barty, that's the problem. High school is where we learn all this stuff. You missed it, and you're lost."

He wanted to swear. It seemed he missed all those learning experiences that would help him deal with other people. So now he was completely useless, and no matter how much he studied or tried to learn, the one being he understood most was Penelope. Even he knew that was pathetic.

"So help me. You excelled in all that."

"I can't do that. What you do has to come from you. But think about what you want to do."

"What I want is for him to say that he likes me and that we can date and go out a few times each week, he'd kiss me, and then after a few weeks, he'd take me home and we could have sex." He was not telling his sister that he'd never had it before, or she'd never let him live it down. "See, that's easy. No muss, no fuss, and everyone knows."

"Where's the mystery and romance in that? If you know everything that's going to happen, then there's no surprise."

"Duh…." To borrow from some of his students.

"The whole purpose is to be surprised and to let someone else like you and do things for you. A guy you're dating shouldn't need to make an appointment weeks in advance like one of your grad students. It doesn't work that way. And let me say that you'll be glad for a little spontaneity. Falling in love is one of the most amazing experiences anyone can have, so don't obsess or fear it, but embrace and go for it." She sighed. "And since you're so clueless about these things, don't equate sex with love. Take your time, because sex is best when you're in love."

"I know all about that. I'm well aware of the body's reactions."

He heard a long-suffering sigh weave through the phone. "You're the smartest person I know and yet you sometimes say the dumbest things. Love isn't about hormones or physical responses. It's more than that, and it will be a learning experience for you. Just don't analyze it too much."

"But what if I'm happy as I am?" Barty asked, and got another of those sighs.

"If you have a feline fetish and Penelope is willing to go along with that, by all means, knock yourself out. Heck, why don't you get a few more cats and you can be like Mrs. Feldman down the block. Remember her? No, I don't suppose you do. She died just before Nana did. She lived alone all her life, had cats, and when she died, they had to round all of them up and the eighteen kittens they found in the house. Is that what you want?"

"No."

"Then whatever you decide, enjoy it and don't get all angsty over it." He heard a wail in the background. "Anna is getting up from her nap, so I have to go. But have fun." She hung up, and Barty set his phone on his desk, wondering what he should do. Calling Jim seemed like a good idea, and maybe they could talk.

His office phone rang. "Dr. Halloran."

"Barty, it's Jim. We got another message from our shooter. Can you come out here? Take the train and I'll meet you at the station. We really need you to listen. He called my voice mail and left the message directly." Jim sounded anxious. "You're mentioned in the message."

Barty went cold. "Me?"

"Yes. Take the train out to the station and call when you get close. I'll be there to meet you and bring you here. Do you have classes to teach on Fridays?" Jim spoke faster.

"No," Barty answered.

"Then pack a bag and put Penelope in a carrier if you have one. Then get the two of you to the train and get here. You can stay with me for a while."

"I don't understand."

"You will when you hear this. I'd come and get you if I could, but we're working like crazy here on this message. Can you promise me you'll do as I ask? I'll explain everything when you get here, and for God's sake, don't go anywhere alone if you can help it. Wait...." He set the phone down, and Barty waited. "Just get here as fast as you can."

"Okay," Barty said and hung up. He packed the papers he was planning to work on for the next few days, put a note on his door that office hours were cancelled for the rest of the week, and made his way out of the building. He'd driven in because of the dreary weather, so his car was waiting for him in his faculty spot, and he raced the rain to its cover. Barty made it home, hurried up to the apartment, and went inside, closing and locking the door behind him. Penelope wound around his legs, and he lifted her into his arms, carried her to the bedroom, and pulled the cat carrier from the closet.

Instantly, Penelope turned into the cat from hell. She clawed and wriggled until Barty got the door open and her inside. Then he closed the door, and she turned her back to him and sat with her butt pressed to the carrier door.

"You never do that." He got some cat treats and put them inside. She ate them and then turned once more in a kitty huff.

He set the carrier on the bed and grabbed an overnight bag. He packed a few changes of clothes and his Dopp kit, then gathered supplies for Penelope. Once everything was inside, he grabbed his jacket and put it on. With his overnight and work bag containing his computer in one hand, Penelope in the other, Barty left the apartment, locked the door, and hurried down the stairs to the nearest train station a block away.

Penelope was not happy, and neither was Barty or the other people in the train car. She yelled the entire ride, sitting on the seat next to him. He called Jim to let him know he expected to arrive in ten minutes, and as soon as he stepped out onto the train platform, Jim met them, took the carrier, and peered inside.

"That's enough out of you. Daddy is doing this to keep you safe!"

Silence, blessed silence.

"The car is right over here. Get inside and I'll bring you up to date." Jim strode across to the car, and Barty kept up and got in the front seat. At least this time he didn't have to ride in back. "Sorry about all this, but we thought it best that you be nearby. I'll play the message for you when we get back, but the shooter specifically mentioned you, by name. So we thought that maybe you might know the man from somewhere."

"How would he know I was working with you unless he was watching? And if that's the case, then we should narrow our search. New Cynwood is a pretty small community, correct? People are tight-knit, and everyone knows everyone, pretty much. It's a typical society, country-club-set type of area. So a stranger poking around is going to be noticed, especially if he's getting access to roofs. But if the shooter was someone everyone was used to seeing, they wouldn't think twice."

"That's true. So you think it's a local person."

"Why would someone from the city or another area start shooting people here? There has to be a connection or something from the town that turned his ire this way. I know it's so much more comfortable for people to think of threats coming from outside. A break-in is so much easier for people to understand than the maid who has been working for them for twenty years walking off with a piece of jewelry. She's thought of as family of a sort and is trusted."

"Our theory was that it was someone who resented the area's affluence." Jim felt a little stupid as soon as he said it. He'd been doing exactly what Barty had described.

"Look closer to home. People don't travel that far for their violence. It's usually close to where they live and what they know. Our shooter knows this town backward and forward, including which doors are locked and where he can get easy perch access. If that's true, then he would have seen me with you the other day, and all he'd need to do was figure out who I was and he could put things together."

"It isn't like the shooter doesn't know we're looking for him," Jim said.

"So you're looking for him, and he's watching you." Barty shivered as Jim pulled into the station. The thought that he was being watched freaked him out completely.

Jim parked and carried Penelope into the station. "I have the same conference room for you, and I thought you could let Penelope out as long as we kept the door closed," he said, and Barty put his things inside, closed the door, and opened the carrier. He also set out Penelope's bowls and a portable litter pan for her. She decided that her carrier was just where she wanted to be and stayed right where she was. "Let's go."

They closed the door behind them, and Barty followed Jim into the captain's office.

"I apologize for putting you in this kind of danger." Captain Westin put his phone on speaker and dialed into the system. Jim entered his voice mail pass code, and then the same distorted voice came through the speaker.

"You really are no closer to catching me than you ever were. But I understand your need to bring in help. Dr. Halloran is probably a good choice, but even he isn't going to be able to help you. I do know what to do if he gets too close. Bang! I'm well aware of what you're doing, and I have eyes in many places. You're going to need a miracle to catch up with me. I'm already many moves ahead." The recording ended, and Barty turned to Jim.

"He called me Dr. Halloran."

"Is that all you're worried about? He directly threatened your life. That's why Crawford here offered to have you stay with him, so you'd have protection and wouldn't be alone. And all you're concerned about is your title?"

"No," he said, turning toward Captain Westin and answering his question. "First thing, no matter what he says, he does know of me or at least my reputation, and it's rattled him. Otherwise why bring me up at all. He called me doctor because that's my official title, particularly in academia. People outside that world rarely refer to academics as 'doctor.'"

"So he's an academic," Jim said. "That could help narrow things down immensely. Do you think that's a red herring?"

"No. He left the message on the spur of the moment. He was trying to disguise his voice, but those devices only do so much. If I were to guess, I'd say he was worried and scared that he might have left some clues or a trail that I might be able to pick up on." Barty thought a few minutes. "Let's go over things again. We may be able to learn something based on this information."

"All right, but I will not put a civilian in danger," Captain Westin said forcefully. "You must stay with Crawford and do what he says." He turned to Jim. "If you think he's in direct danger, you get him out of here and away, even if that means getting him on a plane. I will not have another death that I can prevent."

"Thank you, but I'm capable of taking care of myself," Barty said.

"I'm sure you are, but this is a police matter, and by bringing you into this case, we've also exposed you to danger."

"At the moment, this is blustering," Barty said. "It's the equivalent of a crank phone call. He doesn't think he's providing you with any new information, and he's trying to have all of you running in circles." He sat in one of the chairs. "I understand being concerned for my safety and that of the public, but don't you see that by acting the way you are, you're playing into his hand? He's being manipulative. It's what this guy does."

"And when he doesn't get what he wants, he shoots people," Captain Westin said.

"Yes, he does. But he also wants very much to be in control, and right now we're taking that away. He knows I'm working with you, so he's probably aware that I'm trying to get into his head. His pattern of behavior may change, but he also knows his chances of discovery and capture have increased."

"Just because of you?" Jim asked.

"Remember, our shooter is driven by ego and the belief that he's smarter and better than everyone else. But you brought in an expert, someone he seems to know, or at least knows of, and feels could be a match for him."

"So what do we do?" Jim asked.

"Change nothing. Let him know that he isn't going to get the better of us, and then we'll see how he reacts. I know you'll think I'm crazy, but taking a little control is probably a good thing."

"And if he starts shooting people…?" Jim asked.

"I don't think he's going to do that. He now has an opponent that he thinks is worthy of him, so he's going to want to play his game. Let's let him make his next move, and we'll keep looking for the things we know about him." Barty alternated his gaze between them but looked at Jim a lot more. "Can we expand our research? I know you're looking at chess clubs and things like that, but let's look at professors with strategic disciplines. This is someone who's used to looking ahead, so maybe strategy, military disciplines. He's obviously a good shot. Even economics."

"You're kidding," Jim said.

"No. They are always looking ahead, building models to try to think as many steps ahead of the current economy and consumers as possible. They also try to explain how people behave with money and other factors, so that's not as far-fetched as it may seem."

Jim looked beat, and Barty wanted to help, but each of his ideas only added to Jim's workload.

"We'll see what we can do," Jim said and pulled open the office door. Barty stood and followed him out. "How much of all this is really just spinning our wheels? I mean, we can gather as much information as we want, but with nothing to reference it to, it's just information, piles of it."

"I don't know." He looked at Jim as though he'd gone nuts. "I'm not an expert at solving crimes—that's what you do. I'm only trying to give you insight into where to look. If what I'm telling you isn't helpful, then say so and I'll go away for a while and you can solve your case, and then I can go back to my boring little life with only my cat for company." Where did that come from? The stuff from his sister must have worn off on him, and she must have hit closer to home than he thought. "I know it's a big city and there are a number of universities, but based on the way he talked, it's someone who works or teaches at one. And maybe the chess thing is valid as well."

Jim turned away. "This whole case is frustrating. There's no pattern to what he's doing. Usually we look at the victims to see if there is something they have in common...."

"Detective...." An officer hurried up to Jim, breathless. "I found someone who might have seen our guy. His name is Roger Billings. He owns the shopping center across the street from the last shooting location. He said he saw a man about six feet, maybe thirty-five or so, in a jacket and dark jeans exiting out the back of the building a minute or so after the shooting. He said the man was carrying what looked like some kind of fishing pole case or something. He said he didn't rush or hurry, but walked away from the scene as though he belonged there and knew where he was going. Unfortunately he didn't see what car he went to, because after that, there was all the activity with the shooting itself."

"Why didn't he come forward before?" Jim asked.

"Mr. Billings is in a wheelchair and on oxygen, and he went into the hospital with an infection right after the shooting. He's feeling better and stopped me on my patrol through the area. He said he'd come in if we needed him to."

"No, I'll go talk to him. Thank you." Jim turned to Barty. "Stay here, please. I'm going to take this statement, and I have some other work to do, and then I'll take you home and you can get settled." Jim left, and Barty returned to the conference room.

Penelope peered out of the carrier when he came in and slowly ventured out. She settled on his lap, watching the door. "Are you looking for Jim?"

Penelope gave him a low meow and then settled down to wait.

JIM CAME back about an hour later. Penelope jumped down and wandered to the conference room door, then sat and waited for him to cross to the glass door. Barty picked her up so she didn't run out as Jim came inside.

"We may have gotten a break. It looks like our shooter was seen at least for a few seconds, and we know how he carried his gun in and out."

"The fishing pole case?" Barty asked.

"Yeah. This is the first really huge break we've gotten so far, and it's pathetic." Jim flopped down in the chair with a huff. "We should have gotten further."

"What about the aerial pictures?"

"That was a bust. We got a few samples, and as we suspected, there is no way we can see to that level of detail. We have lots of ideas and very little in the way of putting them into practice. Granted, what are we going to do, photograph everything constantly and then wait for a bullet casing to appear, if it ever does? Like you said, this guy is smart, so he'll probably change his routine."

"What kind of description did you get?"

"A man, about six feet, wearing dark street clothes, probably to blend in. He carried the case, and the only reason Mr. Billings even remembered the guy was because he has a funny way of walking. He said that maybe he'd been injured at some time, but he wasn't sure. It wasn't a limp exactly, but he favored one leg. Mr. Billings said it was how he used to walk before he was confined to the chair—he has MS."

"That's interesting," Barty said.

"How does that fit into your theory?"

"I'm not sure." Barty put Penelope down now that the door was closed, and she wandered around before rubbing against Jim's legs and then jumping into his lap. The scene could have been domestic if they hadn't been sitting in a conference room in a police station. "It could be that his physical condition is putting a time squeeze on his ambitions, and if they were thwarted, again and again, it could add to his frustration and push him over the boundary of rational thought all that much quicker. I'm really trying here, but I think you expect me to be able to think the way he does, and all I can give you is my best opinion."

"I know."

"We have to figure this out before he kills again, and while he's playing with us now with the phone calls, he's going to get bored and make another move. We have to stop him before another innocent person is shot."

"I know that," Jim snapped and put Penelope down on the floor. "Do you understand what I've been going through?" He paused, and Barty could see him steadying himself. "The first shots we investigated as individual shootings, and it wasn't until the pattern emerged that we realized what we were dealing with. We wasted all that time before we figured out what was happening, and then with the last one, we were sure and brought you in to help. I'm spinning my wheels here, and I'm about to ask the captain to see if the FBI can help. Maybe I'm in over my head and it's time to turn this over to someone else."

"Does anyone know this case as well as you? And there has been progress. At least you have a description. I know it's going to be hard, but you have something to go on."

"Yes, and we've already put out an APB with the description, but it's way too vague. If he could have seen just a little more, it would be helpful." Frustration rolled off him, which Barty understood because he felt it as well. Barty wanted to be able to help, and he wasn't sure he was really being of use. He could give him theories and ideas, but not hard facts, and that was what Jim needed.

"Some cases take longer to crack," Barty said. "But you will. I know it." Penelope jumped into his lap, and he stroked down her soft fur, the action soothing his raw nerves. He tried not to think about the message or the fact that the shooter was aware of him. Concentrating on that was playing into his hands, and Barty didn't want to do that. Jim was trained to be cool under pressure, and this case was getting to him. Barty supposed that was natural and all. He wasn't trained in that way, but he liked to think he was level-headed. He snorted. Yeah, right. That coming from a man who hated to drive because of the stress of rush hour. Okay, so he didn't handle pressure well, but he also wasn't going to allow his thoughts and actions to get in the way of real progress. He had to keep his mind on what was important. "Why don't you finish up what you need to and follow up on the things you've done, and then we can go to your house." Barty was getting tired, and he needed a quiet place to think.

Jim left the conference room without another word, and as soon as the door closed, Penelope wandered over and sat in front of the door, watching Jim at his desk and following him with her gaze whenever he moved about the station. She wasn't happy when he stepped out of sight, and Barty had to admit he wasn't either. He liked watching Jim, and his mind wandered to what Jim would look like without his shirt on.

He wanted to slap himself. This was not the time or the place to be having those kinds of thoughts, but time and place didn't seem to have much control over his lustful notions.

"I'M READY to go," Jim said almost two hours later, coming into the conference room and taking a seat. Penelope had climbed onto one of the other chairs and gone to sleep. She immediately woke and scolded him for taking so long. "She's very vocal, isn't she?"

"Not usually, no. I think it's you." At home they were both quiet and had their routine, which had now been upset in a large way. Barty gathered his work together and put his computer to sleep before packing it away. He wasn't particularly happy about this relocation. He would much rather be going home, but he understood they were concerned, and he had to admit he was most likely going to be safer at Jim's, behind alarm systems with his own personal police officer nearby.

"Well, let's get going."

63

Jim was feeling down, and even Barty could sense it. Barty knew he wasn't good around people, but what surprised him was how well he seemed to be able to understand and read Jim's expressions and feelings.

"You know this isn't your fault," Barty said.

"Yes, I do. But I also know that four people have died and I haven't been able to catch this guy."

Barty tilted his head slightly as he thought about what Jim said. "You're the lead person, but the entire team is trying to figure out who is doing this. It isn't you alone."

"I know, but that doesn't really help." Jim looked up from where he'd been studying his shoes and then stood. "We may as well go. Sitting here feeling sorry for myself isn't going to solve this case for me." He helped Barty gather Penelope's things, and when the time came, she went right into her carrier without a peep. "Does she always do that?"

Barty shook his head and showed Jim the scratches from earlier. "I'll need to put something on these. Cat scratches can get infected easily."

They left the conference room, Jim gathered his things on the way, and then they went out to his car.

Penelope seemed happy enough on the ride, and as soon as they were in Jim's house, she cried to be let out. Jim opened the carrier, and she darted out and around the corner.

"We need to find her. This place is big enough that she could get anywhere."

"I bet she'll be fine," Jim told him, and sure enough Penelope returned, winding around Jim's legs. "Maybe she has a kitty crush on me."

"She's not the only one" popped into Barty's head, and he had to keep the words from crossing his lips. Nicole was right—he needed to talk to Jim, because there were things he didn't understand and they were going to drive him crazy. Like the last few hours at the station where he'd sat in the conference room with papers to read for his students and yet hadn't been able to take his gaze off Jim sitting at his desk. Instead of reading about theories on psychosis, he kept thinking about how Jim's arms stretched his shirt as he moved. Jim was attractive—well beyond attractive: he was hot, superattractive. That wasn't the problem. It was Barty trying to figure out if he should do anything about it, and if so, what?

Of course, the entire time all this stuff had been running though his head, he'd been staring at Jim, and now Jim was staring back, and Barty was getting more and more flushed by the second. He'd have said he felt like a teenager, except he wasn't really sure what a real teenager felt like since he'd missed out on most of that sort of thing.

Jim didn't say anything, but he didn't turn away either. Barty licked his lips because his entire mouth had suddenly gone dry, and Jim did the same. He couldn't read the expression in Jim's eyes because it was so foreign to him, but it sent a renewed jolt of heat through him and he really didn't know why.

"I should see about something for dinner," Jim said after a few seconds, and Barty knew he should turn away but couldn't make himself do it.

Penelope broke the connection between them with a demanding yowl. Then she jumped on the table, batted his hand with her paws, sailed to the floor, and blinked up at him like he was supposed to understand what she wanted.

"Okay. If Uncle Jim will show me where I can put your stuff, I'll feed you."

She turned and raced out of the room, and Barty followed her. He found Penelope in the kitchen, sitting near one of the corners, waiting for him.

"I guess she picked her own spot," Jim said.

Barty got the bowls and put down food and water. He put the litter box in the washroom off the kitchen and showed Penelope where it was. She immediately christened it and then wandered back to eat.

"She's a little nuts."

"Takes after her daddy, I guess."

"I don't think you're nuts," Jim said. "Maybe a little different."

"That's a nice way of putting it." Barty had heard much worse in his life. He was usually able to shrug it off, but there had been times when it hurt.

Jim opened the refrigerator and pulled out some things for salad, as well as a pasta dish. "I don't really cook much. My mom and dad have a cook, Regina, and she makes some things for me and brings them over from their house here in town. I know it sounds really spoiled, but if she didn't, then I'd just eat out all the time, and she won't hear of that. Regina has been around my family for years, and she would never let any of us starve." He put the container in the microwave and then began cutting things up for the salad. "So what do you do for fun?"

Barty shrugged. "I work and read a lot. Mostly papers and the various journals. I need to keep up on the latest developments. I, of course, do research, and that takes a great deal of time and effort. I think that's what I like the most because it allows me to figure out some of the things about people that always baffle me." He sat at one of the stools, watching Jim work and staying out of the way.

"No. I mean for fun. My sister rides horses, or she used to. I played polo when I was a kid, but I don't do that any longer. I didn't really enjoy it too much." He placed the lettuce in small bowls and added cucumber and tomato. "Sorry, I went off on myself."

"That's okay, but I don't do things like that."

"Don't you play games?"

"You mean like those time-wasting things on Facebook?" Barty shook his head.

"Some of them are awesome. But I was thinking of video games and things like that."

"I didn't play much as a kid. I didn't have a lot of friends, and I didn't understand how to make them, so I did other things. I can play the piano and the violin. I write a lot and I read."

"But don't you do things with other people outside of work?" Jim asked, and Barty shook his head. "Then you were serious the other day about not having friends? I thought that maybe you were exaggerating a little or something."

"Not really. I find it hard to relate to most people."

Jim carried the salad to the table and got out plates, glasses, and silverware. Then he pulled the pasta out of the microwave, and the scent of tomatoes and garlic filled the room. Barty's stomach growled a little as Jim set the casserole dish on the hot pad. He put the serving spoon in it, poured cold water from a pitcher into glasses, and then sat down.

"There are some times that I wish I was more like everyone else."

"I don't. If you were, then I never would have met you." Jim served him a portion of pasta and then took some for himself.

Barty picked up his fork but didn't eat, wondering just what Jim meant by that. Nicole had said to watch him, and Jim seemed to be watching Barty in return, but he wasn't clear on exactly what all of it meant. He was definitely leaning toward asking, but he was also afraid to find out in case all the energy and heat that seemed to be going on between them was just his imagination. This was all so confusing.

"No, Penelope," Barty scolded when she tried to climb in his lap. He pulled a chair away from the table, and she jumped on it and curled into a ball. "She usually sits with me when I eat. Penelope never begs or anything, but it's part of our routine." He hoped it was all right. Jim didn't seem to mind, and Barty began eating his dinner.

They were quiet as they ate. Barty wasn't quite sure if it was the uncomfortable kind or not. Jim seemed tired and introspective. He could understand that, and it wasn't as though Barty was particularly comfortable. He was in a strange house and was expected to spend at least a couple of nights, from what he could deduce. It had been a while since he'd slept away from home, and the last time had been on a visit with his family where he'd stayed in a hotel and hadn't slept much at all because of all the strange noises around him.

"Are you going to be all right here? I have a guest room made up, and it's near my room."

"How many bedrooms does this house have?" Barty asked.

"Six. I put you in one that has its own bath. Some of them share one." Jim continued eating and seemed distracted.

"What do you do with all this space?" Barty asked. "It's a lot for one person."

"Cavernous is more like it. My grandparents loved it, and they threw great parties here and raised their family in this house. I don't know what I'm going to do with it long-term. My sister would like to move her family here, but her husband has no interest, and she feels that since she's family that I should just give it to her rather than selling it to her."

"Overenhanced sense of entitlement?" Barty asked.

"To say the least. You'll get a chance to meet them on Sunday if things work out. If I dared, I'd hope for some sort of incident so I would have an excuse to stay away, but then that would mean something bad had happened, and I don't want that either. These things with my family are never particularly pleasant."

"Why? My family tries, but other than my sister, they don't really understand me at all. I'm this smart person who intimidates them, and they intimidate the hell out of me."

"I'm going to take a page from your book. Why?" Jim asked, snickering.

"Because they say one thing and mean something else all the time. It's part of how people communicate—I know that. But it doesn't help me figure out what they mean. They say things like 'isn't that a nice shirt' and then look at each other in such a way to say that they think I must be colorblind to wear that. And they think I won't notice. I do, but I don't always know what it means, so I'm always left out. I got used to it a while ago."

"I understand. I get the same reactions from my family about my job. They tolerate it but never talk about it, as though it's an embarrassment to them. They do the same thing to me with the snide undertones, so I ignore it as best I can. The only reason I'm going to this party is because of Deidre's kids. They would miss me if I wasn't there. They're amazing girls, and I love them to death."

Barty finished up and carried his dishes to the sink. When he returned, Jim was done as well, so he took his dishes too.

"Thanks." Jim left the room, returned with the mail, and sat at the table to go through it quickly.

"Why are these addressed to P. James Crawford?" Barty asked when he saw one of the labels as he sat back down.

"James is my middle name. My first name is Pierpont." Jim paused, and Barty put his hand over his mouth to hide his smile. "Yeah, I know. It's a family name, and my dad insisted on it. My mother hated it and always called me Jim. Thankfully it stuck, but in school, every fall it would resurface. I thought about changing it, but now I just put everything as P. James and let it go."

Barty snickered.

"I bet the kids had fun with your name as well, Bartholomew," Jim teased.

Barty shrugged. "I didn't spend much time around the other kids. I moved through school much quicker than they did, and by the time I was fifteen, I was finishing high school and going on to college-level education. That was hard, because I needed a good school and there were none near my parents. I thought of going to school here and staying with Nana, but she said I needed to attend the best schools possible and I needed the scholarships I was offered. Instead, I ended up going away, alone, at sixteen. I wasn't the only one that age, and we had extra supervision because we were still underage and all that. The other kids became friends, but I stayed on the outside as usual, and worked. When I was seventeen and Nana died, I was devastated, but the relationship with my parents had improved, thanks to Nana, and they helped me until I was an adult. It felt like she was still looking out for me."

"So you were twenty-three when you got your doctorate?"

"Yes. I found out I had a gift for understanding the criminal mind, and I was able to use that to get my degree and a fellowship position that turned into a full-time faculty position at Dutton."

"Are you tenured?" Jim asked.

"Not yet. But I've published a lot and publish more all the time. It's one of the things I think I excel at. I like teaching my students, and I try to be understanding. But I also lay out what I expect at the beginning of the term, and I'm very specific and clear because I never like to bend the rules. If I can stick to them, then I'm being fair to everyone."

"I heard you the other day after I left. When you gave that girl an exception."

Barty blushed. "I never know what to do at times like that. So I try to avoid such situations."

"I thought you were gracious and did the right thing, if that helps." Jim put his mail aside and stood. "Why don't you bring Penelope and come with me."

"Where are we going?" Barty asked even as he gathered his little girl and carried her into the other room. Jim sat on the floor in front of a huge television, and then he turned it on. "I thought we could play some games."

"What kind of games?"

"Video games." He handed Barty a plastic steering wheel. "This is an oldie but a goodie. It's a racing game, and I'll help you get set up. You don't have to worry if you lose or die or anything. This is just for fun."

"Can't I just watch you play?"

"No. You're going to play with me. I have the other controller, and we're going to have fun." Jim got everything set up and then helped him set up a character. "You can be whoever you want."

"The turtle, then, because I'm probably going to go as slow as anything."

"Okay." Jim set that up and then showed him how to work the controls. Once he was done, Jim started the game, and it counted down before starting. All the other players raced ahead of him while Barty hadn't even started. "Just go forward like I showed you and pick up speed. Stay on the track and weave around the obstacles."

"I'm terrible at this." He wanted to give the controller thing to Jim, but he continued around the track. "Okay. This is kind of fun," he admitted just as the race came to an end and he came in last. Barty handed the controller back to Jim. "I think I'm done."

"No. Try it again. I'll set it to replay, and don't be afraid to go faster. Nothing is going to happen if you crash, other than you start up again. It's only a video game, not a real highway."

He went through the motions, and this time he came in tenth. "I beat them?" Barty asked, pointing to the ones lower on the list.

"Yeah. Now do it again." Jim reset it once again.

This time Barty was more aggressive, shooting around the other drivers and letting go. He laughed and might have whooped a few times when the others crashed, but he came in third and was thrilled.

Jim high-fived him and everything. "You never had anything like this as a kid?"

"No. Only educational things. Can I do it one more time?" He was ready to go, but this time it was a new track and he only did all right. "This is sort of fun, but kind of mindless." He passed the control back to Jim, who ignored him. "You're being pushy."

"And you're acting scared of a video game," Jim countered with a gentle smile that took the sting from his words. Barty didn't understand why he knew that, but he did, and that made it all right. "And being mindless is part of the purpose. What do your studies tell you about play in adults?"

"That it's good stress relief and helps them cope with the harder things in life. People need downtime."

"And you're a person and so am I. So there's nothing wrong with having a little mindless fun."

Jim started the track again, and this time Barty was having a ball. He'd sort of forgotten about the other things around him, and when on his sixth race, he came in first, Barty jumped to his feet, and Jim did the same, hugging him.

Barty stilled as he wondered what had happened. Jim was still holding him, and when Barty lowered his gaze slightly so he could look into Jim's eyes, he asked, "Is this a friend thing or a something else thing?" Barty was feeling warmer by the second. He inhaled and almost moaned as Jim's intoxicatingly intense, musky scent filled his nose. He was getting hard, and if this was just a friend thing, then he was going to have a difficult time looking Jim in the eye in about two seconds because it was going to be obvious.

"I don't know what it is," Jim said, releasing him, taking a step back, and wiping down his face. "If it would have been someone else, like Garrett"—Jim cringed slightly—"I probably would have said it was more than that. But I don't know what you want, and...." Jim sat back down. "Shit... let's just play. I was happy that you did so well, and we should leave it at that."

Barty was totally confused, but he sat back down and tried not to let the blood ringing in his ears get to him. Jim had simply overreacted, and maybe he didn't like him the way Barty thought he might have liked him.

Not that Barty would have expected a guy like Jim to be interested in him anyway. He was a freak of nature. His intelligence and abilities were rare in anyone, and they came with a price. He liked that he was smart, but there were so many times he wished the price for that intelligence hadn't been so high. Sure, he could read a thick book in less than an hour and absorb everything in it in a single read, recall it, and rework it to fit his own arguments. Then he could store it and recall the information years later. Nothing ever left him, so during an academic argument, he could bring in obscure facts and figures to back up his position at the drop of a hat. That was the positive side, but the negative was that he didn't make friends or understand the reactions of other people outside his textbooks and academic pursuits, which made him even more of a freak—a professor of psychology who didn't understand people.

At least he had his answer and didn't have to wonder what Jim thought.

Penelope climbed on his lap, and Barty watched Jim come in first in his race, then handed him the controller.

"We can play together."

"I think I'm ready to go to bed," Barty said softly, the fun having gone out of the game.

"Barty," Jim said. "I didn't mean to upset you. I just got a little carried away with the hug."

"You think that's what upset me? You hugged me, and it was nice. No one touches me. I haven't been hugged or anything in a long time, unless my sister counts, and somehow I don't think she does. I guess I'm not the kind of person that people think romantically about, and that's okay."

"Is that what you wanted? I thought I'd scared you and gone too far."

Barty groaned. "Just because...." He didn't know how to say this. "Just forget it, okay? We don't have to have this conversation." He wasn't going to try to explain that he'd been hoping that Jim liked him that way. That he'd been watching him the entire time they'd known each other. All Jim had done was hug him in a moment of happiness. Nothing more. He was the one making a great big thing about it, and now he felt like a fool.

"Come on," Jim said, handing him back the controller. He switched the game so the screen split, and they were racing each other. Barty knew he wasn't going to win, but frustration was a great motivator. He waited for Jim to start the race, and then Barty shot out the starting gate and onto the course. This was the same one he'd raced first, and he knew every turn now, so he gunned it and was prepared for the tricky spots. His memory came in handy, and he went as fast as he could, not caring if he wiped out. All he wanted was to beat Jim. He was ahead, but then Jim passed him. Then Barty caught up and passed Jim, only to have Jim pass him once again. The game said there was only one lap left, and at that moment, Barty was the fastest turtle on a scooter ever. He floored it, going around the curves, ignoring the skid, and overtook Jim just before they crossed the finish line.

Barty handed Jim the controller. "I won," he said softly.

"What do you want for a prize?" Jim asked, his voice deepening, watching him intensely.

"You don't have to give me anything," Barty said as he squirmed slightly under Jim's intensity. He wondered what he'd done wrong.

Then Jim smiled, warmly. "You did great. Did you have fun?"

"You don't mind that I beat you? Everyone always hates it when I win." Barty had stopped playing games of any type years ago.

"Nope. It's only a game. Why get all worked up over it?" He leaned closer, and Barty swallowed. "Like I said, what do you want for a prize?"

Barty didn't know how to answer, even though he thought he really should have been able to figure it out. He sat back, still staring at Jim. "You're sending me very mixed signals, and I don't know what you mean." He decided to stay on solid ground and go for a more analytical approach. "First you hug me and then back away. Now you're looking at me like I'm lunch and asking me what I want for a reward for winning." Barty set Penelope on the sofa and stood. "Is this a game? Because I don't get it. If you want something, just ask. If there's something you're trying to hint at, it isn't getting through. So please just tell me." He walked toward the door only because he didn't need to see the expression on Jim's face.

"Barty, I didn't mean to confuse you."

"But you did. I don't get people like that. What's left unsaid is foreign to me. Just say what you mean. I won't get mad or upset, but this beating around the bush just makes me confused."

"All right."

He heard the creak of leather and then Jim's footsteps approach from behind. He was about to turn when Jim's hands settled on his shoulders. Barty closed his eyes and soaked in the simple touch of another person. He liked Jim's warm breath on his neck and the heat from Jim's hands as it soaked through his shirt. He didn't dare move because then maybe the touch would retreat and he'd be left out in the cold once again. He wasn't sure what this meant, if it meant anything at all other than Jim trying to soothe him. But he wanted it to last. So he practically held his breath just so he wouldn't move a muscle and bring the moment to an end.

Barty slowly turned because he couldn't stand it any longer. Jim's gaze caught his, and Barty gasped softly as the light of understanding dawned. God, he hoped he was getting whatever message Jim was sending right. Barty flushed, and heat welled under his clothes as he became more and more sensitive. Jim moved closer, lightly guiding him forward until their chests touched. Jim's hands slid off his shoulders and down Barty's back, drawing him more firmly to Jim's embrace. He tilted his head, Barty did the same, and they closed the gap between them. A kiss, warm and firm, spread even more heat through Barty. The hold increased, and Barty moaned softly, moving his lips slightly while letting Jim lead the way. It was incredible, and his head felt floaty and wonderful, the musk he'd smelled earlier intensifying as the taste of food and Jim sent his tongue on a dance of joy. He wanted more, but he wasn't quite sure how to ask for it. Still, he got it. Then Jim backed away slowly, and Barty blinked as though he needed to make sure it was real. The kiss had been sublime, special, amazing.

Their kiss. His first kiss.

"Is something wrong?" Jim asked, and Barty realized he'd been staring off into space like he was on some sort of cloud. He smiled widely, and Jim chuckled. "I'll take that as a no."

"Good choice," Barty said.

"See. Games are fun, especially when you win."

"Yeah. But…."

"As adults, we need to play too. Maybe sometime I can take you to a playground. Well, an adult-type playground."

Barty lowered his gaze. "I've already been to that kind of playground, and I don't think I ever need to go again. It was disgusting, and some guy asked me if I wanted to give him a—" Barty lowered his voice. "—blowjob." He said it the same way older people say the word cancer. "I told him no thank you and left as fast as I could." Barty felt like giggling but refrained. "I mean, I might have thought about it, but it was a creepy place, and eww. I mean, who knows where his bits had been. I'm picky about my food, let alone things like that."

"I wasn't referring to places like that, but since you brought it up, why did you go there?"

"I was young, just an adult, and I wanted a magazine. I wandered into the other part, and then that man asked me that, and I turned and left without getting anything and never went back. I found the bookstore in the Gayborhood after that and got what I needed there. It was safer and less creepy."

"Is that where you've gotten your information about sex?" Jim asked.

Barty grinned and shook his head. "You can't do anything in my field without dealing with sex. I've read textbooks, sex education materials, stories, seen some movies—you name it. I've just never actually had any myself that involved another person." God, that was so embarrassing. He remembered the guys in college talking about it when they didn't think he was listening. Maybe if he'd had some friends, he might have been able to do more, but things were the way they were.

"Well, I'm glad you got out of there and didn't do anything. You could have caught something that stayed with you for the rest of your life," Jim said. "Besides, I like that you're a little innocent. It's attractive and kind of sexy."

Barty didn't think that was true, but he wasn't going to call Jim a liar. Especially when he kissed him again and Barty pretty much forgot about the stuff they'd been talking about. Heck, he nearly forgot his own name and what he did for a living, and that was the best feeling he could ever remember. When the kiss ended, his second kiss, Barty held his breath once again, this time just so he could file the memory away in a place he could never forget it.

"I really should go to bed." If he didn't, he'd likely throw caution to the wind, rip off his clothes, and rub naked all over Jim like an oversized cat, but the whole rubbing and meowing thing was Penelope's bit. The whole naked thing with Jim sounded like an amazingly good idea, but he knew, academically, that caution was the best course of action, so he reluctantly backed away. "Please," he added in a whisper almost low enough that if Jim didn't hear him and pressed it, he knew his resolve, already shaky at best, would shatter.

Jim nodded but didn't say a word. He didn't move either, and Barty stayed still as well, the pull between them ebbing and flowing with each breath they took. Part of Barty really wanted Jim to take him upstairs, leading him by the hand, to Jim's bedroom, strip him down, and show him the best time of his life. He wanted it badly, but he was afraid of it too. It was new, and Barty never adjusted to new things very well. New academic pursuits were awesome; other things, not so much.

"Come on," Jim finally said, breaking whatever it was between them. "Wait, your bag is still in the car. I'll go get it."

Barty nodded, unable to speak for fear of what he'd say, and Jim turned, deactivated the alarm, and went outside. Jim returned less than a minute later, closing the door, resetting the alarm, and making a call at the same time it seemed.

"Yeah, I need patrol cars to my house now. There is someone watching the house. ... I don't know. ... Be sure to tell the captain it could be related to the shootings. ... No sirens—we want to catch this guy if we can." Jim hung up and turned to Barty. "Turn out the lights, then go upstairs and turn on the light in any of the bedrooms. I want whoever is out there to think we've gone to bed."

"Okay." Barty began turning out the lights.

"Just leave Penelope. She'll be fine," Jim said, and Barty continued turning off the lights and then went up the stairs, turning on lights and then turning them off again as he moved. He chose what looked like the first bedroom at the top of the stairs, turned on the light, and went inside. The room was stunning, with dark wood, light walls, a huge king-size antique bed that looked fit for royalty, and enormous furniture that glowed in the soft light. Everything from the fireplace to the gleaming floors and plush rug said wealth, status, and luxury. Barty hoped this was the room he got to stay in at least for a few nights. Penelope was going to feel like the queen in this room. Barty shook his head as he realized he was thinking about his cat at a time like this.

"Go down to the end of the hall and turn on the lights in the last room on the right," Jim said softly, probably from the top of the stairs.

Barty did as he'd asked. That room was just as amazing, maybe more so, with its carved fireplace mantel and wall lined with rich wood paneling around it. This was Jim's bedroom; Barty had no doubt about that for a second. The room was clean, the bed made, but it smelled like Jim: earthy, rich, musky. Barty sat on the edge of the bed and waited for what Jim asked him to do next. His heart raced, and he wanted to go to the window to see what was going on outside, but he knew that wasn't a good idea, so he sat where he was, wishing Penelope was with him so he wouldn't be all alone.

Barty strained to hear voices as they came up the stairs and drifted down the hall. There were definitely other people in the house, but he couldn't hear what was being said. He left the room, keeping the lights on, and slowly walked to the top of the stairs.

"What were you doing hiding in my bushes?" Jim asked, but Barty didn't hear an answer. "Fine, take him to the station and book him on suspicion of murder. He certainly fits the description we have."

"Now wait a minute. I didn't kill anybody," a strange voice said, and Barty went down the stairs. "That's the guy who's up to something," a strange man in dark clothes said, pointing at him. "I was hired to follow him and find out if he was cheating on his wife. I saw him come out of the police station with you...." He looked like the quintessential bumbling private eye on television, wearing old black clothes complete with a hole in his shirt near the pocket.

"And the camera?" Jim asked, holding up the large lens.

"My client wanted pictures," the man explained, glaring at Jim.

"Show me some ID, now!" Jim barked in full cop mode.

He took out his wallet and handed Jim a driver's license.

"Willard Samsone." He looked at Barty, who shrugged. Then he handed the license back.

"You have to be the dumbest private dick on the face of the earth," Barty said. "If you'd have done your homework, you'd have known I wasn't married and that this is the home of a police officer." He stepped forward. "So cut the crap and tell him the truth and who you're working for." He was so angry, he wanted to hit the man, and he'd never struck another human being in his life. "How dare you decide to follow me."

"That's what I was told, but I thought it was bullshit. Still, I was paid to follow you and report back with pictures."

"Who paid you?" Barty demanded in a growl, and Penelope added her own indignation, swatting the man with her claws, and he jumped back with a yowl.

"I don't really know. The job was through e-mail, and the money was sent electronically. I don't question things too closely. He had a job for me, and I was paid."

"I want every e-mail you have." Jim turned to the other officers. "Take Willard to his office and get whatever he has. And check him out thoroughly."

"You can't do that," Willard groused. "I know my rights."

"Then lock him up. He can sit in jail for a while. You're a person of interest in a murder investigation. I'll be in tomorrow to talk to you. In the meantime we'll find you a nice, comfortable cell with a very interesting roommate."

"Wait," Willard said nervously as Barty took a second to smile at Jim's use of psychology. The last thing this guy wanted was to spend time in jail, and somehow Barty didn't think this man had anything to do with the man they were after. The shooter was way too smart to hire someone like this. "I have a copy in my car, the glove compartment."

"Go take a look," Jim said to one of the officers while the other stayed with Willard.

Barty took a few steps back, and Jim came over. "I don't think this guy is working with the shooter. He'd never hire someone, because everything has to be done just right. This man is way too sloppy and not too bright."

"I agree, but why does someone have a detective following you?" Jim asked. "If it isn't him, then someone fed this guy a line so that he'd follow you."

Barty shook his head, trying to think, but came up with nothing. "I don't have any idea. I'm just a professor, and I live with a cat."

"Is there something you haven't told me?"

"No. I don't know what's going on." He took a step away at Jim's harsh tone. He didn't like the way Jim was talking to him at all, and it made him angry. "I don't have anyone in my life, and the only people I see during the day are my colleagues and the students. You know, last time I went to the grocery store, I went through a different checkout line. Maybe the regular lady got jealous and wondered why I wasn't seeing her?"

Jim stared at him blankly, like Barty had gone around the bend or something. See, that was why he didn't try to relate to people. They never understood him.

"That was my attempt at sarcasm."

"I see that. It wasn't bad, but not much help."

Thankfully the officer returned with a few printouts. "We can see if we can trace this address through the service provider," he said and handed the printouts to Jim, who looked them over and then showed them to Barty.

"I think the client's a woman," Jim said. "Look at the address. Littlepony3."

"I haven't done anything wrong," Willard said.

"Fine. Get all his information and go to his office. See what you can find on this client. We need to know for sure that this isn't related." The officers led Willard outside, and Jim closed and locked the door. "There has to be some reason why someone would hire a detective to follow you."

"I don't know," Barty said again. He hated that Jim didn't believe him, and he wasn't going to stand here and argue. What a way to completely ruin the extraordinary feelings of a first kiss, with private detectives and a dose of suspicion. "Can I go upstairs to bed now?" He wanted to get away and be alone.

Barty left the foyer and found Penelope curled on the sofa in the spot where Jim had been sitting. He picked her up and returned to the other room, where he got his bag and carried it to the top of the stairs, waiting for Jim to show him which room he wanted him to use.

Jim followed, then led the way down the hall to the room across from his. Jim turned out the lights and closed the door to the first room Barty had gone into, then pushed the door open to the other room. It was nearly as nice as Jim's, with its warm, substantial furniture.

"The men tended to sleep at this end of the house and the ladies on the other. The bedrooms down there are much more feminine. I didn't see any reason to redecorate them. You can look tomorrow if you want."

Barty went inside. "Thank you," he said and closed the bedroom door. Then he put Penelope on the bed and sat on the edge. He was angry and hurt. He and Jim had had a fun evening that had ended with his first kiss, and somehow that had morphed into suspicion. That wasn't at all how he'd envisioned this moment.

At a soft knock, Barty got up and opened the door.

"The bathroom is right through there. There's a cupboard with towels and anything you might need. My room is just across the hall, so if you need anything…."

"Like a dose of skepticism," Barty said. He couldn't help it. The words just slipped out.

"It's my job to ask why and try to figure out the reason for things. It's how cases are solved. I believe you when you say you don't know why you were being followed, but the fact is that you were, and the only person right now who might have any answers is you. And I don't want to try to protect you from our shooter only to have someone else slip under the radar."

Barty was only partly mollified. "Who would want to follow me? I bet if I wasn't involved with this case, Willard would have followed me for two days and then nearly died of boredom." There were times when his own life seemed tedious even to him. But Barty tended to stick with what he knew and what was safe. Then he didn't get hurt or rejected by people. "I'll see you in the morning." Barty closed the door, grabbed his bag, and carried it into the bathroom, which was palatial with rich dark cabinets, gleaming stone tile, and a huge claw-foot tub. Penelope wandered in with him, jumping up on the vanity counter, staring at him with her huge blinking eyes. "You think I was hard on him?" Barty asked, but of course Penelope only sat there. She never had any answers for him.

He cleaned up and got ready for bed in a pair of light sleep pants and a Dutton T-shirt that they'd handed out at a staff function earlier in the year. Then he left the bathroom, turned out the main light before switching on the bedside one, and climbed into the mammoth bed. There was room for two other people at least in this thing. Barty ended up getting out of bed again, opening his door slightly so Penelope could leave and reach her litter box and bowls. Then he got back into bed, turning out the light. Penelope joined him a few minutes later and curled at his side. Barty couldn't help wishing it was Jim.

# CHAPTER 5

IT SEEMED that no matter what leads they managed to dig up, they went nowhere fast. A witness might have actually seen the shooter, but the description was so vague that there was little to go on. Even the insights from Barty, while good, were of limited help. They were going through university professors and staff, but the task was turning out to be nearly impossible since there wasn't a single database they could search to come up with a list of people who met that description. After all, this wasn't television where databases of teachers, chess clubs, and anything else they wanted were readily available. The only good thing was that there weren't any more incidents or phone calls.

Jim and Barty had been through all the material they had to date and were still coming up with very little.

"Where could this man have learned to shoot like that? They weren't easy shots," Barty said.

"We thought about military training, but unless we have more to go on, the simple fact is, we have very few things we know for sure about this guy. Even what you've told us are guesses. Granted, I tend to think you're right, but we still don't know." Jim was beginning to think the best thing that could happen was another shooting—hopefully unsuccessful—but it would give them a chance to catch him.

The captain had stepped up foot patrols in the community to try to deter the shooter. Jim wasn't sure it would help, but the public had to be reassured and a visible police presence was the best way to do that. Everyone was on alert and on edge, watching for the slightest thing out of the ordinary. The number of calls from citizens was way up and needed to be investigated, and Jim spent all day Saturday and Sunday morning doing that, each time hopeful that he'd stumble on a clue, some piece of information that they needed, but each time he had his hopes dashed.

"Go home and get some rest," Captain Westin said after lunch on Sunday. "You're wearing yourself out and you're going to need your energy. A little birdie tells me that you have a family to-do today, and I know this case has you worked up, like the rest of us. I'm not telling you it isn't important, but you need a little time away to let things settle. You and Barty have been working long hours." Captain Westin was about to leave and then turned back to him. "He's really working out."

Jim sighed. "I think so. I think he understands this guy really well."

"You're worried about him," Captain Westin said with a look that had Jim wondering just how much he might have guessed about Jim's feelings for Barty.

"Starting yesterday he's been quiet and staring at statements and every piece of evidence. And just a few minutes ago, he was sitting in the conference room, Penelope in his lap, absently stroking her like a Bond villain, while he looked at nothing. I'm not sure what's going through his head, but I'm wondering if he's getting too close to this."

"He's a civilian, not a trained police officer, and it's possible he's working too hard or trying to get into this guy's head and what he's finding isn't pretty. You're going to have to watch him and if necessary provide him with some distance." He sounded genuinely concerned. "Now go get him and take him home. I think you both need some time off."

He left, and Jim took care of what he'd been working on. Then he stopped by the conference room to get Barty. He was still sitting still, thinking.

Jim pulled the chair up next to him. "What's going on?" he asked gently. "I know you're deep in thought, but you haven't said much in the last day. What are you thinking about?"

"Everything," Barty said without turning toward him. "I'm trying to think like the shooter, and the more I do, the more I wonder if he and I have a lot in common." Barty turned to him, pale, and his eyes wide as though he'd been shocked. "I keep putting myself in his shoes, and last night I dreamed that I had climbed onto a roof and placed a bullet casing. It was the same one we first visited, and then I returned and stared down the barrel of the gun at a person on the street. I woke up shaking, wondering if he could be me, or I guess if I could be him. I have all the classic signs and fit the profile for someone like him."

"But you aren't," Jim said. "You didn't climb to the roof and take the shot, and I'm concerned that you may be getting too involved. You can't get too close."

"But it's the only way I can help. What I do is try to learn how people think, but this man thinks a lot like me, I know it." Barty continued stroking Penelope, but she tired of it and jumped down. That broke some of the spell that Barty was under.

"The captain wants us to go home and get some rest. I have that party at my sister's."

"You were hoping to work so you didn't have to go, weren't you?" Barty smiled. "You told me as much a few days ago. But it looks like you'll have to go."

"And you can come with me," Jim offered.

Barty nodded slowly. "I don't do well at parties and things. But I'll go with you if that's what you want."

"You don't have to," Jim said, even as he was happy Barty had agreed to go. "It's a garden party, so we need to look nice but don't necessarily need a shirt and tie."

"Like I said, I'll go with you, but mostly because I don't want to be at your house alone. What if whoever hired the detective shows up?"

"We're trying to figure that out." But at the moment, since it didn't seem related to the shooter, their resources were stretched and it was one of the things Jim wanted to have an officer look into. "We have a request into the service provider, but often they won't release any information without a warrant, and someone hiring a detective isn't considered probable cause. I really doubt the detective himself is going to cooperate too closely. He doesn't want to give up information on his clients, or he won't have much of a business."

"So someone was following me and I don't know why," Barty said. "I really just want to go home, but then I wonder if there will be more people following me or a shooter watching me."

"It's all right. You're with me, and I'm going to do everything I can to keep you safe. I promise." He took Barty's hand. "I know I messed things up the other night and I should have been more sensitive and less demanding."

"I really don't know why someone would follow me. I'm so boring."

"We'll get to the bottom of that, but for now I don't want you to worry about it. Let us continue to look into it, and you let this shooter go for a little while and just concentrate on having a little fun. My sister will have great food, and everyone will be talking. It's what they do at things like this. I suspect there will be a lot of academics there, so you'll have plenty of people who'll have things in common with you." Jim looked out into the station and then back to Barty. "Let's go to the house so we can change and get ready. It will be fine, I promise."

JIM TURNED onto his sister's street and pulled over before reaching her house. "You have nothing to be nervous about." He took Barty's hand. "Everyone will be polite, and you're someone new, so they'll be interested in you." Jim leaned across the seat as Barty nodded. Jim touched his chin, and when Barty turned, Jim kissed him. "I've wanted to do that since the other night. But I wasn't sure how you felt." He realized he probably messed up with Barty.

"I didn't understand how you could just turn on me like that. I never lie about anything with anyone. It takes too much effort, and when you lie, you have to remember the lie so you can continue the story. I don't think it's worth it. So it hurt when you didn't believe me." Barty swallowed, his right leg bouncing up and down. "A few minutes before, you had given me my first kiss, and then you accused me of lying."

Jim was floored and sat back in complete surprise. "Your first kiss? You mean no one had ever kissed you before? Not even in college?"

Barty shook his head.

"Not even once?"

"No. Who would want to kiss me?"

Jim leaned forward, cupped Barty's cheeks, and kissed him. "I would. And I'm sorry for acting like a real jerk. I do that sometimes when I'm in work mode. It comes with the territory. In order to get answers, sometimes I have to push, and I went into that mode with you." Jim was beginning to understand that Barty might be really smart, but in some

85

ways, he was rather fragile. His near-complete lack of any relationship experience left him feeling vulnerable and unsure of himself. Jim, on the other hand, was attracted to Barty but still cautious. His past relationships had all ended badly, and they were all professor-type guys like Barty. Not that he really thought Barty was going to treat him the way Garrett had, but it took some effort to let that go because it was always in the back of his mind. Barty wasn't Garrett. In fact, he was about as different from Garrett as it was possible to get. "It wasn't like I didn't believe you. I just needed you to try to think. Lots of times people know things they aren't aware of."

Barty nodded. "Okay. As long as you believe me now."

"I do. I always did," Jim said and turned back so he could drive once again. "At the party I'll introduce you as a colleague. There will probably be a lot of speculation about the shootings because it's too close to home for them not to."

"I'll say nothing. I'm pretty good at that," Barty said, and Jim put the car in gear and approached his sister's home.

He pulled into the circular drive, parking so he could exit easily if he had to, and then they got out. Deidre met him at the door, and she air-kissed him, and then Jim introduced Barty.

"Dr. Halloran," she said with a smile. Deidre was the slight, feminine version of Jim, with longer flowing hair, wearing a floral sundress that said summer and warmth.

"You know me?" Barty asked.

"I know of you, I believe. Some of the others in the department were talking about your paper on pathological behavior, and we were speculating on its connection to economic behavior." She shook his hand. "What's curious is why you're here with my brother." She stepped back so they could come inside.

"We're working together," Barty said.

Deidre flicked a glance in his direction. "On that dreadful shooter case?" She shivered.

"We aren't at liberty to talk about it, and I'd appreciate if you'd keep your speculation to yourself," Jim told her. "It would be very helpful." He glared at her. "I mean…."

"I know, and I'd never say anything." She took Barty's arm and led him through the house and out to the backyard, with Jim following behind. In his family's eyes, that was his place now.

"This is Dr. Halloran," she said as she entered the yard, and a few people seemed to recognize him. Jim stayed close and saw Barty try to shrink away. A few of Deidre's colleagues that he'd met before introduced themselves, and Barty exchanged pleasantries.

"Why don't you come with me? I'm sure your friend will be fine for just a few minutes," Deidre said, and they weaved through the tables topped with white tablecloths and chairs draped with covers and pads. Each table had sprays of flowers, and there was a bar under the far end of the tent where many of the people congregated. "I didn't know you were going to bring a guest." She glanced away, and Jim followed her gaze to Barty. She actually sounded pleased. "You should have told me. To have such a distinguished friend."

"Be nice. I know what you think of me, but you can be nice to him."

Meghan and Mindy hurried across the yard to him, and he turned away from their mother. "Uncle Perpy," they cried in near unison, in adorable floral dresses similar to their mother's.

Jim wanted to strangle his sister for telling them his real first name.

"Hi, sweeties," he said as he hugged and kissed each of them. "You're both getting to be such big girls."

"See, I can do this," Meghan said as she twirled around in her party dress.

Mindy tried and would have fallen if Jim hadn't caught her.

"That's great, honey." He hugged them both again, and they took his hands and led him away, chattering like little angels. "I think I'm supposed to stay out there with the grown-ups," Jim said when they tried to pull him inside the house.

"Girls, go on and play with Colleen for a while, and I'll call you when it's time to eat," Deidre said. She insisted that the girls have a nanny, saying she worked too much and she needed help.

Personally, Jim would rather spend time with the girls than be out at the party, but he figured it was time to rescue Barty and make sure he was okay.

"I'll see you at lunch," he told them and got another hug before they were escorted inside by a college-age woman. Jim then went in search of Barty, Deidre already mingling with the other guests. Her husband, Franklin, was near the bar with the other men and seemed to have been drawn into whatever conversation Barty was involved in. Well, he was involved because he seemed to be listening, but Jim figured he wanted to get away and wasn't quite sure how to do it.

"How are you doing?" he asked Barty quietly.

"Okay," Barty answered.

"So are you tenured yet, Dr. Halloran?" one of Deidre's colleagues asked. It took Jim a second to remember his name.

"Not yet, Stewart. I haven't been there long enough yet. Almost four years. I'm on a tenure track, though." Barty seemed more uncomfortable by the minute. "I teach a number of graduate-level classes, and I've published three or four articles a year so far."

Instantly Stewart went a little green around the edges. "You publish that much?"

Barty nodded, and Jim could feel him withdrawing quickly. He had to step in.

"Barty works very hard at what he does, and he's working with us in order to get some additional information for his research. I'm Deidre's brother, Jim. I think we met at her Christmas party."

Stewart shook his hand, and Jim saw the light go on. "You're the police officer."

"Yeah. Jim is great," Barty said, staring down Stewart, with his narrow blue eyes, until he backed away.

"It looks like you're having a good time impressing everyone," Jim said once Stewart had decided he needed another drink and went to the bar.

"He doesn't like me very much," Barty said.

"Not surprising," Deidre said from behind him, and Jim jumped a little. She turned her back and lowered her voice. "Stewart is a very smart man, but he expects everything to come easily to him and does the minimum to stay in everyone's good graces."

"I'm sorry if I said something I shouldn't have," Barty said.

"You didn't. He was fishing to find out where you were in relation to him on the academic food chain. He just found out you're a whale and he's a feeder fish. Please don't worry about it."

"Is everyone from your department here?" Jim asked.

"Good God, no. Well, I did invite everyone because it was polite, but Mason Gardener isn't here yet. He's the one I beat out for department head, and he's still smarting a little." Deidre moved closer. "He has a huge ego, and it got a little bruised, but he doesn't publish as much as he should and the other faculty don't like him. He always thinks he has the answers." She turned to Barty. "I'm sure you have one of those that you work with. If he'd work a little harder, well, he and Stewart, they could each make a real name for themselves, but they're both worried about how things look rather than getting results."

"Maybe we could work on something together," Barty offered. "I'm willing to bet that there are definite overlaps between some of my pathological models and some economic models. How do compulsion and pathology drive economic spending?"

"That could be amazing and quite new," Deidre said. "I'll definitely call you in a few weeks when I have some things cleared off my plate, and we can map something out."

"See. She likes you more than she does me," Jim told Barty once Deidre had stepped away. He was being sarcastic, but in a way, it was true.

"I don't know about that. I mean, we work in the same field, sort of. And we have things in common. Besides, from the looks of things, your sister is in her element… and she gets to be queen bee. I'm sure that had something to do with it."

"I hear you teach psychology," a man said as he approached. "Mason Gardener." He held out his hand to Barty.

Jim tensed as he realized this was the man Deidre had beaten out for the position they were all here to celebrate. Mason certainly had brass nuts, that was for sure. Jim had been introduced to him a few times, but they never really spoke. He looked at home in the setting, in his perfectly pressed tan slacks and expensive cobalt blue, short-sleeve shirt that rippled in the light.

"Barty Halloran. I'm a professor of psychology," Barty said levelly. "What do you do?"

Jim put his hand gently at the base of Barty's back just so he would know he was there.

"I'm a professor of economics at Templeton. I'll be working under Deidre, at least for a while," he said, turning to Jim.

"Gardener, you made it," Deidre said as she joined their little group. "I'm so glad you came. Did Franklin answer the door and explain where everything was?"

He nodded slowly. "I have a family get-together in a few minutes, but I wanted to stop by and say that there are no hard feelings." He smiled widely, and Jim actually went from looking at Mason to Deidre. The tension between them was palpable, and for a few seconds, he reveled in it.

"Of course not. We've worked together for years, and we'll continue to do so," Deidre said graciously, but Jim knew her well enough to know she was only tolerating Mason because she had invited him and he was here. "Can I get you anything to drink? We'll be serving a late lunch in an hour."

"I have to go soon. My brother is having a cookout with his kids. But I did want to stop by."

Deidre motioned to the bar and told him to make himself at home, and then Mason caught the eye of other people at the party and moved away. Jim and Barty found themselves momentarily alone.

"How long do we have to stay?"

"As long as you like," Jim said. These things were a little dull for him. "We can meet my parents," he said, and they moved over to where they were just entering the yard. "Mom, Dad, this is Barty Halloran."

"Do you work with Jim?" his mother asked from under a white sun hat decorated with summer flowers that matched the ones on her dress.

"I am at the moment." Barty shook hands with both of them, and they talked about nothing for a few minutes. Then his buttoned-up-to-the-throat father excused himself after only a few words to him and joined some of his other friends. His mother talked briefly and then excused herself as well. "If they weren't your mom and dad, I'd like to kick both of them in the keister. They talked to me more than they did you."

The girls hurried out of the house to see their grandma and grandpa, and Jim did his best not to grind his teeth in frustration. Things were the way they were, and he'd come to realize there was nothing he could do about it.

"Most of the time we barely spoke. This family are experts at denying what they don't want to see." Jim stepped up to the bar and asked for a double vodka. He downed it when it was delivered and asked for another. He didn't want to get drunk, but he could certainly deal with a slight buzz right about then. This was why he didn't like to come to these things.

"So, son," his father said from behind him. At least he'd loosened the top button on his lime-green polo shirt. His father looked like he wanted to get out of there as fast as he could so he could hit the course. At least that's the impression Jim got from the plaid pants he wore.

"You're going to talk to me?" Jim said. "I figured you had decided that I didn't exist at the moment."

"There's no need to make a scene," his father whispered and asked for a whiskey. "You have your life, and I can accept that. But that doesn't mean I have to allow that sort of behavior to influence my life." His drink was delivered. "Booter, how's the golf game?" his father said, moving away as though Jim wasn't there at all.

Barty had found some more admirers, it seemed, because once again he was surrounded by Deidre's various colleagues. Jim moved off to one edge of the lawn and sipped his drink. He'd known coming here was a mistake, and he hadn't wanted to come at all. The funniest thing was that Barty had been worried about coming because he wouldn't know anyone and then, boom, he's the life of the party and Jim was on the outs. Granted, he was happy that Barty had people to talk to, but he was also a little left out.

"Uncle Perpy," Mindy said, pulling on his pants leg. "I'm bored. Will you play with me?"

Jim set down his glass. He'd had enough to drink, and this little one was a reminder of why he'd come in the first place. "Sure, honey. Did you see Grandma and Grandpa?"

She nodded. "Grampy was grumpy, and Grammy said she needed to talk to the ladies." She pushed out her lower lip, and it was all Jim could do not to smile.

"I know a game. Why don't you go over there and rescue Mr. Barty?" he asked, but she shook her head. She was normally a little shy around strangers. "How about if I come with you?"

"Okay." She took his hand and led him to where Barty was starting to look like he could use a drink.

"We came over to say hello," Jim said, and Barty turned.

"We're here to rescue you," Mindy said and took Barty's hand. "And go play ponies," she added, and Jim knew they'd been had.

Barty was gracious and let her lead him toward the house.

A shot rang through the air, echoing off the house and through all the partygoers. Jim hit the ground, pulling Mindy down and under him for protection. Barty was right next to him. "Get her in the house now," he told Barty, and as he moved forward, a second shot added to the confusion. Jim turned just in time to see dirt and grass fly up into the air next to him. "Everyone inside, now!" Jim cried. "Get in the house. Barty, call the police, tell them I need backup." Jim raced for cover, even as he looked toward where the shots had come from. The property was lined with high hedges on a berm for added privacy. Jim drew his gun from under his summer jacket and raced off, ignoring the screams and cries of the others behind him as they all tried to get through the doors into the house at once.

He knew the house and grounds, as well as the neighboring property. He'd visited both before, so Jim cautiously made his way over, using the house for cover as much as he could. He opened the gate near the side of the house, staying low to the ground, and peered down the other side of the hedge. It was empty. Of course. Jim ran out toward the street as a black sedan pulled away from the house. Jim raced after it. The road only turned right at the corner. Jim sprinted across the huge corner lot, jumping immaculate hedges and shrubs, cutting off distance, pointing the gun at the side of the car, a bead on the driver, finger on the trigger.

"Stop," he yelled at the top of his lungs, adrenaline pumping as he was about to shoot.

The car came to an abrupt halt, and he raced up. "Get out with your hands up," Jim called, racing to the driver's side. The door opened, and Jim's first indication that something was wrong was when a small, tan-shoed foot in heels gingerly reached for the ground. It was followed by the rest of the woman, who was old enough to be his grandmother. Jim holstered his weapon and walked up to her as she stared at him with wide eyes.

"You can have my purse, just don't hurt me," she said, shaking.

"I'm sorry, ma'am," Jim said. "I'm a police officer. Are you all right?" He felt like a fool, making a rookie mistake. "Did you see another car pass you?" He breathed to steady himself.

"No one passed me. But another car pulled out as I was coming up the street."

"Can you tell me what it looked like?"

Sirens sounded, getting louder with each second.

Her shaking had stopped, and she held the side of the car.

"Do you need some help?"

"I'm perfectly capable of caring for myself when men aren't pointing guns at me," she snapped as she slowly got back in her car. "The other car was blue, dark blue, but that's all I saw. It was a car, though, not one of those behemoths," she said, pointing to the huge SUV in a nearby driveway.

The sirens grew closer. "I'm sorry again, ma'am. Could you please pull over and wait a few minutes?" The police cars came to a stop, and Jim waved an officer to him. "Get her statement," Jim ordered and raced back toward his sister's house.

"What happened?" Captain Westin asked as Jim met him getting out of his car.

"Two shots fired. I don't think anyone was injured. I stopped the woman over there as she was pulling away from the scene. I doubt she's the shooter, but she might have seen the car."

"Go around back and make sure everyone is all right," Captain Westin told him as he headed for the front of the house.

Jim hurried the way he'd come through the gate. Tumbled chairs littered the lawn, a few of the tables had been upset, their bright flowers trampled into the dirt. No one was outside lying on the ground, which was good. Jim approached the back door, and it opened for him, and he stepped into pandemonium.

"All right," Jim said over the din. "Is anyone hurt?"

"No," Barty said from one of the chairs with Mindy on his lap, hugging him. She squirmed down and hugged Jim's legs. Deidre approached, handed Meghan to Jim's mother, and picked up Mindy, comforting her gently. "I already checked."

"We'll need to speak to each of you before you leave," Captain Westin said. "So get comfortable, and we'll let you go as soon as we can."

People continued talking in hushed tones as Captain Westin made his way over to Jim.

"Did you see where the shots came from?"

"The neighboring hedges," Jim answered, pointing to the side of the yard. Then he and Captain Westin stepped outside and beyond of the view of the people in the house. "One of the shots hit near Barty. I saw the dirt fly from the second shot. I think the first also hit nearby."

"So you think he was the target?" Captain Westin asked, and Jim nodded once.

"I can position us in the yard. We'll need to see the trajectory of the first shot to know for sure." His mouth went dry.

"Okay." Captain Westin got officers into the backyard to secure and process the scene. "I want you to work with them out here. I'll talk to the people inside."

Jim nodded and joined the two officers.

It was easy enough to find where the second bullet was; the divot was clear. But the first one was more difficult. Jim searched, looking over every inch of grass, and then moved to the hedge.

"Over here," one of the other officers, Jones, called from the bushes behind him, just down the hedgerow, and Jim hurried over. "Look at this," Jones said as he pointed to privet leaves from the bush, scattered on the ground.

"That's from one of the shots," Jim said, peering back up the hole. There were marks on some of the branches inside the thick plant. "Get pictures of everything and carefully dig the bullet out of the hedge." His sister was going to kill him for ruining her perfect shrubs, but it couldn't be helped.

He turned and followed what he hoped might be the trajectory of the second shot across the yard and into the hedge on the other side. "Here is where he took the shot," Jim said, being careful not to touch anything. He leaned down, looking back toward the spot in the other hedge. In his mind's eye, he added where he and Barty had been standing, and some things became very clear to him. Barty had been target of at least the first shot. The second one was much lower and nearer to where they had been on the ground, a further attempt.

Jim walked over to where they'd been, not touching any of the evidence but looking at where they had been and then at the shooter's spot. The coward had taken a shot at Barty while he'd been on the ground.

"What do we have?" Captain Westin asked as he approached Jim, stepping around the evidence markers while the officers continued gathering evidence and taking pictures of everything.

"One bullet in the hedge over there and one right here. Barty was standing here." He pointed so he didn't disturb the ground any more than it had been.

"I have a forensics team on the way, so put markers where you and other people were."

"Yeah."

"We're processing the scene, but I'm not particularly hopeful. No one seemed to have seen anything. The hedge is thick enough that they couldn't see through it, and people were coming and going, so it's hard to know if anyone slipped away. But did you notice anyone leave the party just before the shots were fired?"

"Not particularly. I was with my niece and Barty when the shots were fired. I didn't hear anything and made my way to where I thought the shots had come from, but I saw no one, and—"

"Yes. Mrs. Hodges explained how you two were introduced." He didn't say any more, and Jim kept his mind on the task in front of him rather than on his ever-growing concern for Barty. "She told us about the car that passed her, but it came from farther up the block behind her."

Jim swore under his breath. "It's my guess that the shooter went back through the other yard and then out to the street. And judging by the caliber of bullet recovered, the weapon was a handgun this time."

95

"So the MO has either changed or we have a different shooter. The others were distant and detached. This one is much closer and seems more personal. It could be whoever hired this personal investigator, but I doubt it. I put more pressure on the guy this morning, and he did offer that he thought his client was a woman. It took some arm-bending and a little negotiation, but he also agreed to contact her and find out what her real motives were."

"Why would he do that?" Jim asked, but Captain Westin simply stared at him for a few seconds.

"Let's just say that I like Barty too." He took a step closer. "I need you to step away from this investigation and my crime scene now. Let us do our jobs. You need to give a statement just like everyone else before we can let people go. Then, once we're done, I want you to go home for the rest of the day. This is going to take quite a while."

"I'm off the case?"

"No. But in this instance, you're a witness, and I need you as that more than I need you personally involved at the moment. Get some distance, and once they're through with both of you, get Barty home, and for God's sake, be careful. Someone certainly seems to be out to kill him."

Jim turned and went inside. A number of people from the party had been cleared and were gone. The officers used Deidre's study as a command post and called in witnesses one at a time. Jim sat with Barty and waited his turn. Deidre and Franklin were nowhere to be seen, and neither were Jim's parents.

"They went upstairs with the kids," Barty told him when he asked. "Meghan was upset, and Mindy kept saying how you held her when the big booms sounded. She is so cute." Barty's words expressed he was trying to make light of things, but his eyes said he was terrified.

"It's okay. No one was hurt."

"I know. But he was after me," Barty told him. "He as much as said so in his last message, and I discounted it."

"We don't know who it was," Jim said, but Barty shook his head.

"I know it was him. There is no doubt in my mind."

"What about whoever hired the detective?"

"You mean the most bumbling man on the face of the earth? Please. Whoever hired him didn't know what they were doing at all and hired the cheapest guy they could find. No. That's a red herring. I mean, please, the guy almost peed himself when you threatened to put him in jail. No. That's someone who wants to know something about me, not the shooter."

"We shouldn't talk about this here," Jim said, checking to see if anyone was listening to their conversation. They didn't appear to be paying much attention to either of them, and Jim moved closer and put an arm around Barty's waist. In the thick of things, he'd thought of catching this guy and making sure Barty was safe. There had been a backyard full of people, and while he'd yelled for them all to get inside, the one his mind and heart had gone to was Barty. To think that the preliminary evidence suggested that Barty was the target made him shake inside at how close he'd come to losing him.

His own fears and past be damned. Jim was downright afraid for Barty's life. Hell, if the guy had shot at Jim, it would have scared him less than Barty being the target. And it was his fault that had happened. He was the one who brought Barty into this mess, and now it was his fault that Barty was in the line of fire. Jim was damned sure as hell not going to let it happen again.

They called Barty in, and Jim sat nervously the entire time he was gone. It went on for quite a while, and Jim knew they were trying to figure out if Barty had any enemies and all the usual lines of questioning. Once Barty came out, he looked bruised and was moving rather slowly.

"Come on, Jim," Captain Westin said, and Jim stood and took his turn in the hot seat. "Did you discharge your weapon?"

"No," Jim answered, then went into his explanation of what happened. "Do you have people checking the neighborhood?"

"Yes, Jim," Captain Westin said. "We know our jobs and are spreading the net as wide as we can, and you'll be in the loop once we're done processing this scene, but for now, you're a player, a part of the crime scene." They went over his movements and what he saw and heard. "Is there the possibility of a third shot? A few witnesses thought they heard one."

"No. There were two. Because of the stone house and the berms, the yard can echo. The girls and I play with it sometimes. It does it in spots, but I wasn't in one of those and it was clearly two shots."

"And they were both close to Barty," Captain Westin asked.

"Yes. As far as I know. I told you where we were in the yard."

"Where was your niece?"

"Mindy? She was between us, and I pulled her down under me with the first shot, to protect her. I needed her safe. She's only three."

"We're working through the exact bullet trajectories now, but it looks like the shooter was on the far side of the hedge and that some of the branches may have changed the bullet angles a bit. Handguns aren't as accurate as rifles, as you know, but you weren't that far away."

"So you're saying you think Barty was lucky."

"It seems that way," Captain Westin answered, and Jim paled and turned away to get some air and himself under control. He felt his worry rise quickly and wished to hell he hadn't reacted that way in front of the other officers. He needed to keep his personal life out of his work. "We need to make sure we catch this bastard fast. I want all work done as quickly and thoroughly as possible. Jim, you'll remain lead investigator, but I'm going to manage everything and coordinate the work in the station. That way we can divide and conquer. This case is getting bigger by the day."

"Thank you," Jim said. He wasn't going to turn down any help he could get.

"Now go on home. I think we've put Barty through enough right now."

Jim nodded and left the room. The house was largely quiet. He went looking for Barty and found him in the living room with Deidre, Franklin, and the girls. They were all huddled together, the girls playing quietly on the floor. Barty sat next to Deidre, talking quietly, and she was listening, both she and Franklin nodding every now and then. Barty didn't know Jim was there so he stayed back. Barty seemed to be helping them, and a lump formed in his throat. He'd been concerned about how Barty was going to be able to handle all this and worried he'd react badly. But Barty was apparently more concerned about Deidre, Franklin, and his nieces than he was about himself.

As Jim watched, little Mindy got up from the floor and tugged on Barty's pant leg. Barty looked shocked, and then he lifted Jim's little niece into his arms, and she hugged him around the neck. When he put her down, she went to her mother and did the same thing, settling there. Meghan seemed less affected, probably because she was inside the house when everything happened and hadn't actually witnessed it.

"I thought I told you to go home," Captain Westin said quietly from behind him. Jim stepped away and let him glance in the room before he too stepped away. "That's not what I expected to see."

"Neither did I," Jim said. "But it's what he's trained to do."

Captain Westin nodded slowly. "Sometimes he seems so… innocent, maybe naïve, to do what he does."

"Barty has told me that he has trouble understanding people, but that's not the case, judging by what I just saw."

"Everyone has their skills, and clearly whatever he's doing is one of them."

Barty was obviously so much more than what Jim had first thought. Maybe Barty just didn't see himself as he really was. But Jim thought maybe he was starting to. He'd begun developing feelings for Barty over the past few days, but the scene he'd just witnessed touched his heart.

"Jim," Barty said, coming out of the room. "I'm about ready to go."

"Let me say good-bye to them, and then I'll take you back to the house," Jim said and went inside. He hugged both of his nieces and held Deidre's hand.

"I don't know who could have done this," she said softly as he looked up from Mindy. "Your friend… is Barty just a friend? Because he's brilliant and knew just what to say. He does understand." She wiped her eyes and then hugged him, something she hadn't done in many years. "Take care of him… and yourself."

"I will," Jim agreed, and she released him. Jim said good-bye to both his nieces, lightly stroking their blonde hair. He joined Barty, and they left the house, telling Captain Westin that they were leaving.

"Penelope is going to be happy to see us."

Jim didn't understand that comment or why Barty was choosing to focus on his cat after everything that happened. They got in the car, and

Jim left the neighborhood, went through the nearest drive-through for some food, and then drove home.

Jim entered the house cautiously, checking that the alarm was truly undisturbed. Once they were inside, he reset all the perimeter sensors and then went into the kitchen. He got plates and mugs and grabbed two beers before returning to the family room, where he found Barty sitting on the sofa with Penelope on his lap.

"If you don't mind my asking, what did you say to Deidre? Because right now you're, like, her favorite person in the world."

Barty didn't move. "I just listened, mostly. Your sister is extremely driven, but she cares very much what others think of her. She was concerned that no one was hurt and then, of course, that Mindy was so close to the shots. I explained that the fear and concern she was feeling were justified and normal for any mother and that she should take comfort that her daughters and her guests were all fine."

"Is that all?" Jim asked and took a bite of his burger. He hadn't realized how hungry he was until he took that first bite.

"No. I told her that she's going to be afraid and that was normal, but I said that her daughters were going to need her and that she had to be strong for them. Your sister has a steel backbone, and all I did was try to remind her of that. I don't know what it's like to have children, but I do know what it feels like to be shot at and missed. What I don't know is how I'm going to feel about it once I have a chance to think. But right now I'm okay."

"I know you don't think you're good with people, but you knew exactly what Deidre needed to hear."

"That's because of training. In the end Nana was right. Going into this field did help me understand people, but from an intellectual perspective as opposed to a personal, deep-down understanding. Sometimes that's a good thing, and other times it's very difficult. I think today it was good. I was able to remain detached rather than get caught up in my own emotions and fear." Barty took a bite of his burger and then set it down, chewing slowly, like he was contemplating something. "They were shooting at me, weren't they? They didn't tell me in the interview, but they asked plenty of telling questions."

"We think so. But until they work out the ballistic trajectories, it will be difficult to tell. Sometimes there are surprises." Jim bit his lower lip, wondering just how much to tell Barty. Until now he'd been very up-front with him. "He shot through the hedge and there are marks on the branches, so it's possible that trajectories were altered. We don't know yet, but it seems like you were the target."

Barty nodded blankly. "Then he's becoming more desperate. This wasn't a distant act, but up close, and I'm not sure how thought-out it was."

"He got away pretty cleanly," Jim said.

"True, but this time he left clues. I'm sure of it." Barty stared at his food but didn't touch it. "You know, it feels funny to be someone's target. For years I was the guy in the corner who people only saw when they wanted something, at least outside the academic arena, and now I have the attention of a psychopath." Barty turned toward him, his eyes hollow, fear pulling at his lips. "I think I'll go back to not being noticed very much."

"I know what that feels like. I was the target in Philadelphia a few years ago. It's why I left the force there and came here. I needed to get away from all that. I was assigned to a gang task force, and somehow one of the gangs got hold of a list of officers on the force, and they targeted all of us. At first it was harassment and things to try to send a message to back off. Then one of the members was shot, and I was being followed a few times. We found the ones responsible and shut down the gang completely in the end. But the family in charge, three brothers, attacked me, and I nearly died from multiple gunshot wounds."

"And then you come out here looking for something quieter and end up investigating a serial shooter who is now targeting the person you're…." Barty didn't finish his sentence. "I don't know what to say here."

"I know, and it's my fault."

"I mean, I know a kiss is just a kiss and it isn't a marriage proposal or anything. But sometimes kisses signal the beginning of something more, and sometimes they're just kisses. I've only had three so I don't have anything else to compare it to, and…. But does it mean something more, or was it just a kiss because you like me?"

101

Jim leaned closer, his food momentarily forgotten at the confusion in Barty's eyes. He tugged Barty closer and brought their lips together. Barty tasted like hamburger, but only for a few seconds, and then his natural richness took over. He loved how Barty tasted and loved the mewling whine that welled up in his throat. It took all Jim's self-control not to make a similar sound.

Then Jim pulled back. "Does that answer your question?"

Barty blinked at him for a few seconds and then shook his head. "Not really. It's a wonderful kiss, but what does it mean?"

"Okay, it means that I like you and think you're someone special. It also means that we're working together and we should be careful."

"But I'm only a consultant," Barty said. "I'm not really part of the police force or anything, and at the moment, I'm here because you're protecting me."

"I'm trying," Jim said, thinking he wasn't doing a very good job. He should have told Deidre that he wasn't going to be coming to her party because of the case he was working on. The girls would have been disappointed, but he wouldn't have put them and Barty in danger the way he had. "Not doing a very good job, though."

"Yes, you are. How were you to know he'd attack people at the party?" Barty asked, and Jim gasped.

"What if he was already at the party? You said yourself that you thought the shooter might work in academia and that there were triggering incidents. What if one of the triggering incidents was my sister being chosen as department head? She was throwing a party and invited all the people in her department, and the shooter was already there and saw you."

"I suppose it's possible," Barty said and then yawned. "I'm sorry. I haven't been sleeping too well, and after all this excitement, I think I need to lie down after we eat." Barty finished his burger and drank some of the beer. "I think you might have a good idea."

Jim nodded, and his first thought was to call Captain Westin, but he held back. It was just an idea, and he had nothing to back it up with at the moment other than suspicion. And he'd been given a direct order to go home and get some rest.

"I'm going to write this down so I don't keep running it around in my head all night."

Barty took what was left of the food into the kitchen, with Penelope following. When he returned, he sat in one of the chairs and pulled the light throw Jim kept on the sofa over him.

"You can go upstairs if you like," Jim offered, but Barty shook his head.

"I don't want to be alone."

That settled it. Jim had been contemplating going in to the station regardless of what the captain had said, but he wasn't going to leave Barty, and they both needed a chance for a little quiet time. He went into the office and sent his ideas and theories in an e-mail to himself. When he returned, he'd hoped to find Barty asleep, but he was back on his feet, pacing the room, Penelope watching him from the chair like she was looking at a tennis match. At least Jim had his answer.

He stood in the doorway, letting Barty pace. Sometimes people needed to work things out for themselves. He wasn't sure if that was what Barty needed right now, but his nervousness was contagious, and Jim's own stomach clenched and his heart rate increased, making him flush.

"They kept asking me if I knew of anyone who might want to hurt me," Barty said. "I told them no, other than the man who'd left the message. I mean, things happen, and there is professional jealousy, but is that enough to take a shot at someone?"

"People have killed for less, but I don't think that's what's going on here, and neither do you," Jim said as Barty stopped pacing and turned to him, looking every bit like a kid who'd lost his puppy.

"Then why did they ask me all those questions? I'm not the killer, and…." He wrapped his arms around himself as if to give himself his own hug. "I don't understand. Even Captain Westin was there, and he didn't stop them."

"They have to go through everything. We can't assume things. What if you'd just had a fight with a colleague and he'd stormed out with threats to make you pay? We'd need to look into that. What if the shooting isn't related to the others? I think it is, but that's speculation that needs to be verified somehow." Jim walked into the room and right up to

Barty, putting his arms around him, and Barty leaned into him. Damn, he felt perfect in his arms. Barty was just a little taller, but at the moment, he seemed smaller and delicate.

"It still hurts knowing people are going through your life to see who might want to hurt you. Not that I have much of a life to go through. It should take them all of ten minutes." Barty lifted his head away so Jim could look at his face. How anyone could overlook Barty was a huge surprise to him. Barty's eyes alone were so big, filled with intelligence and light. Their beauty tugged Jim closer, and he waited for Barty to tense right up until he kissed him.

Jim had meant for the kiss to be light, to reassure, but Barty slid his arms around Jim's neck and pressed harder, deepening the kiss as he shook in Jim's arms. He hoped like hell it wasn't more fear, but from the way Barty pressed to him, clinging and damn near trying to climb up him, Jim knew there was so much more at play.

Jim still hesitated. Barty had only been kissed, and Jim knew he'd never done anything else. The thought of introducing Barty to sex was both heated and nerve-racking. He had to take his time and make it special for Barty, but Jim was wondering if this was the right time to do that.

However, it seemed Barty had his own ideas. "I need to forget," he whispered. "I never forget anything, but today I need to forget what happened, at least for a little while." Barty kissed him as though he were a ravenous wolf.

"We shouldn't have sex, especially your first time, just because you need to forget what happened. Your first time should be more than that." Jim moved away, hoping Barty would cool down a little. He was hard enough to pound nails, and part of himself screamed for him to take Barty upstairs to his room and introduce him to the wonders of sex. But he was not going to have Barty regret anything between them or make rash decisions because he was scared or worried about what had happened.

"Jim, I know my own mind."

"I didn't say that you didn't. But I also know human nature, and this is a reaction to what happened and I won't do that to you." Jim guided Barty back to the sofa and sat him down. "Just lie back and close your eyes." He tugged Barty's legs and feet onto his lap and took off Barty's shoes and socks. Then he slowly rubbed his feet.

Barty groaned softly and lolled his head back on the arm of the sofa. Penelope jumped up and rested on Barty's chest, riding it up and down with each breath.

His feet were soft, and Jim stroked along Barty's heel and down his foot over his toes, then back up and along his calf under the leg of his pants. "How is that?"

"Heavenly," Barty whispered, and Penelope purred. The scene was so domestic and relaxed that Jim was having a hard time remembering the events of a few hours earlier. The fallout and investigation would be there waiting for him when he went into work in the morning, so he was happy for a few hours of peace, and to have them with Barty was an added bonus.

He continued stroking until Barty's eyes began to get heavy, the warmth and gentleness of taking care of Barty lolling him into quiet peace. Barty's eyes flitted open and then closed, only to open once again. Finally they drifted shut, and Jim gently let his hands slip away and placed Barty's legs on the sofa. Once Jim stood, he spread the throw over Barty's legs and left him and Penelope sleeping together.

Jim went to his office and called Deidre. "How are you holding up?" he asked when she answered her phone.

"I'm doing okay." She was about ready to cry—Jim could hear it in her voice. "I worked so hard, and to have the celebration of years of work end like this...."

"It doesn't change how good you are, and none of this is your fault. This happened, and we'll find out who did it." She needed reassurance more than anything. "You do have connections with the police department, after all."

She chuckled, and Jim hoped some of her nerves went with it. "I'll remember that."

"Even if you don't like what I do," Jim said, and she was silent.

"We were wrong, Jim," she said quietly. "All of us. Mom and Dad saw it too. They saw how you put yourself at risk and covered Mindy and then how you took off after the guy while everyone else was hurrying into the house."

105

"That's nice of you to say and all. But it doesn't matter much. That part of things was always a problem everyone else had. I love my job, and I am who I am. I can live with that."

"How is Barty holding up?" Deidre said, and Jim left the office, speaking quietly as he went across the hall to the family room doorway.

"He's asleep on the sofa right now. And you probably don't want to hear this, but he looks like an angel. I know he isn't perfect or anything. No one is, but he's pretty special in his own interesting way." Jim watched as Barty slept on.

"You have this thing for geeky academics," Deidre teased. "This is what, your third one?"

"The first two broke my heart," he admitted. "I don't know if I can do it again."

"Hey. The heart will break and heal as many times as you need it to. That's the beauty of it. Besides, I think Barty is one person who'll break his own heart before he hurts you. Don't know how I know that, but I do. So if you're going to take a chance on anyone, it should be him."

Jim didn't respond.

"Damn it, you stubborn ass. You can rattle around in that house alone for the rest of your life, or you can open your heart and take a chance. We all live with that same decision. So you were hurt—so was I, and I'd take all the heartache of the losers I brought home just so I could have Franklin and know when I had found him."

"You don't understand. The things I've seen families do to one another, not just ours—you have no idea the calls I took years ago. I once found a wife nearly beaten to death by her husband because she overcooked his beans." Jim would never get the image of the woman out of his head for as long as he lived.

"Do you think Barty will act that way?"

"No."

"Then there you are. Don't let our fucked-up family keep you from having one of your own." Deidre sighed. "I have to go. The girls need their dinner, and then we're going to have a story-time evening. I nearly lost one of my daughters. I think Franklin and I need to make some changes in our lives, and they start tonight."

"Good for you. Maybe it's time I made some changes as well." On that note, they ended the call and Jim put his phone in his pocket. Barty continued sleeping, wiggling his nose every few seconds and then swiping at something in the air around him. As Jim continued to watch, Barty squirmed, and Penelope jumped to the floor and walked away, her bed moving more than she liked. Barty rolled onto his side and fell back to sleep, whining and whimpering softly.

"Barty," Jim said softly, going over to the couch and rubbing his back. "It's all right."

Barty shook awake and then rolled over, blinking at Jim. "There were people shooting at me."

"I figured. The crap during the day always surfaces when I'm asleep too. Some nights I barely sleep at all, and others my head is quiet and I can rest."

"How do you make it stop?" Barty asked, sitting up.

"I haven't figured that out yet. I've been shot at multiple times and hit a few. The vest stopped one, and another time I was hit in the leg. I've been cut, scraped—you name it. And so far I've been lucky that nothing has left me permanently hurt. Though sometimes at night, I live them all over again. I guess over time it fades. Some of them have for me, and now the nightmares come less often." Jim sat down. "You asked what helps—being really tired." He took Barty's hand.

"I don't think I'll ever get over being shot at," Barty said.

"Let's take our mind off it for a while." Jim got up and tossed Barty a controller.

"Video games?"

"It's pretty mindless and fun. This is what I do after a hard day. There's nothing like a little play to round out the bad times." He slipped the disk in the machine, and they played a dual game. Winning or losing didn't matter; all that did was letting his head go somewhere other than to shots whizzing around him, screams of fear, and God knew what else. Jim looked over at Barty. He loved his smile, and tonight it was a grin as he whizzed around the track. They played for a few hours, and laughter temporarily replaced anxiety and concern. Jim knew it was only temporary, but it helped nonetheless.

"I really like this game."

"I have others we can play." Jim put in another and taught Barty how to drive a race simulator. It was equally fun. A lot of the games involved shooting, so he stayed away from those. This was to forget, a kind of release from his day. He hoped it would be the same for Barty.

It was late by the time they stopped playing and went upstairs to bed. "Good night, Barty," Jim said outside his door before kissing him. Jim waited until Barty went inside and then entered his own room to find Penelope in the middle of his bed. "What are you doing here?" He lifted her off the bed and put her outside the door. She raced back in before he could close it and jumped on the bed once more, making herself comfortable. "You know Barty's going to miss you." He approached, and she raised her hackles for a second and then settled once again on the bed. "Damn cat." He lifted her off the bed once more, walked across the hall, and knocked on Barty's door. "Did you forget someone?"

Barty opened it, and Jim stared at Barty's bare chest. "There she is." He took Penelope, pressing her to his chest, and went back inside the room. "Thanks, Jim." He put her on the bed, but she jumped down and raced across the hall into Jim's room.

"She's acting weird," Jim said as he returned to his room. Penelope was once again in the same spot in the center of his bed, and Jim swore she was grinning up at him.

Barty came in and leaned over the bed. Just as he reached for her, she scampered away, leaving Barty flat on the mattress, his little rear end up in the air. Jim couldn't help staring and had to look away before Barty turned back around. "What's with you?"

Penelope raced out of the room, and Jim rolled his eyes.

Barty sat up on the edge of the bed. "I don't know what's gotten into her. I'll find her and take her in with me." He hurried out of the room, and a few minutes later, Jim heard the door close across the hall. He closed his own and got ready for bed.

Jim turned out the light and climbed under the covers. He should have been tired, but he ended up staring up at the ceiling, wondering what Barty was doing and if he was okay. More than once he thought about getting up to check on him. He even got out of bed, but went to the bathroom for a drink of water instead. He felt rather stupid. Barty had said he was interested, and Jim had backed off. Now he wished he'd brought Barty into his room. Even if they didn't have sex, it would have been nice to have someone with him so he wasn't so alone. Jim rolled over and closed his eyes.

He was half-asleep when there was a knock on his door. It cracked open, and Barty came inside, the dim glow from the hall light slicing through the darkness.

"Jim."

"What is it?"

"I can't sleep. I keep dreaming about getting shot. I don't know what to do. It won't stop." The unsettled fear in Barty's voice was more than Jim could take.

"Come here." He lifted the covers, and Barty sat on the edge of the bed. "I know what that feels like."

Barty turned to him. "Are you sure?"

"It's okay," Jim said, and Barty lay down. Jim lifted the covers over him and tugged Barty close. Dang, he felt even better in his bed than he had in his arms.

"I feel like such a baby. I should be able to handle this. I'm a psychologist, and I've been trained for things like this my entire academic life."

"Doctor, heal thyself," Jim said softly. "Sometimes we're too close to the things that happen to us. I deal with victims all the time, and I've been told that I'm good with them. But when I was shot, it was different. I've helped numerous gunshot victims over the years, but I was a mess for a long time. Being a victim of a crime is more unsettling than anyone can imagine." Jim closed his eyes, nestling his hard-on against Barty's ass. He didn't really give it much thought. It wasn't as though he could control it.

"I think I can now," Barty said. "You know it's difficult for me to put myself in other people's shoes."

"Yes. But I think that's because your life has been so different from most people's. But you share something with them now. One in three will be affected by a crime. So now you know how it feels."

"I want to catch this guy and rip his arms off," Barty said. "He attacked me and nearly hurt your little niece. When I first began studying psychology, I wanted to learn how to be a better person and deal with others. Then I wanted to learn about myself, and what I found scared me. Because I had a lot in common with them, at least from a psychological standpoint. I used to get so frustrated."

Jim listened as Barty told his story, tugging him a little closer.

"I told you I graduated high school early, but it was a hard time for me, with Nana's death, and before I graduated, the kids weren't nice."

"I can imagine."

Barty rolled over slowly. "I was picked on a lot. I was smaller than the other kids and an easy target. One kid shoved me into a locker all the time. That was frightening. Nana told me to let it go and continue studying. That I would be leaving there soon. She was right, but by the end, I used to fantasize about what I'd do to Milo…. Milo Macaffrey. I wanted to kill him." Barty quivered in his arms. "I remember sitting up at night, thinking of ways that I could end his life. I thought about getting a gun and shooting him. I did poison him once."

"What?" Jim whispered.

"He used to steal my lunch, so I baked some cookies with ex-lax in them. That time, he took my lunch but ended up spending the rest of the day in the bathroom. I didn't feel bad, if that's what you think, and when Nana found out, she was so mad. I told Nana I wasn't sorry, and she sat me down and asked me what would have happened if he'd had an allergic reaction or something. I remember shrugging and telling her it would serve him right. The thing was, I didn't care. He was nothing to me, nothing at all."

"Okay…," Jim said, feeling chilled even as Barty radiated heat. This was a part of Barty he never expected.

"That's when I started studying and learned about people like me. Nana sat me down and explained why what I'd done was wrong and why my reaction frightened her so. 'Barty, honey, if you don't care about other people and hurting them is easy, then how will you get along? You need to be a good person.'

"'But they hurt me,' I remember saying.

"'I know. But you hurting that boy also hurts me,' Nana said. 'Always remember that hurting someone else is also hurting yourself and the people who love you.'" Barty sniffed. "That I understood, because I never wanted to hurt Nana."

"She sounds like an amazing woman." He tugged Barty closer.

"She was, and she had a way of helping me understand these kinds of things. So after that I was always careful around other people. Once I learned about myself, I was extra careful. At least then I knew the cause, but I didn't know what to do about it, other than to consciously put myself in other people's positions. I didn't like getting hurt, so I didn't do things to others that I didn't like. It's strange trying to learn empathy as an adult when most people learn it as a child."

"But you're a good person. I know that."

"I'd like to think so. But I know that this monster is inside me. Well, a potential monster."

"Barty, would you kill someone who pissed you off or got the better of you?"

"No. But it isn't that simple. Whatever is going on in our shooter's mind built up over a long time. Years of resentment, pent-up rage, being given less than what he thought was his due—all of it has built until he snapped. That's what happened to me and Milo. He'd picked on me and pushed me until I sort of snapped. I went to a great deal of trouble, planning to do what I did. I had to get the ex-lax, bake the cookies, and keep track of the special ones. I had to put them in my lunch for a few days until he decided to steal my lunch. I did it coldly, thinking I was in the right. He had hurt me, and I was going to get him back. Thankfully he only got the shits, but it taught me what I was capable of."

"But you know and understand, and I hope you're happy now," Jim said and saw Barty nod in the dim light. Then he felt him move closer, his legs entwining with Jim's.

"I think I am. I have work that I love, and I get to do research. My students are good, for the most part, and I have Penelope," Barty added.

"Is that all you want?" Jim asked in a whisper.

"Sometimes I'm really lonely. I live alone, and outside of work, I don't see many people. My sister suggested I get a cat for company.

Nicole is probably my best friend, but she doesn't live near here."
Barty rested his head on Jim's shoulder. "She was the one who told
me that the weird feelings I had when we first met were because I
liked you."

Jim closed his arms around Barty, lightly stroking up and down
his back. He was so tempted to go lower, to run his hands over Barty's
butt, to press them closer. "Is loneliness all there is… to this?" He'd been
through enough heartache already, and he didn't need still more.

Barty stiffened. "You think I would do this and be with you… for
sex… just because I was lonely? I know how to take care of things…
with my hand. I don't need to have sex with someone just to have sex.
And I haven't been lonely for the last few days because I've been here
with you. Granted, things have felt strange staying here instead of home,
but I think I like it." Barty leaned closer. "I like you."

He closed the gap between them, and Jim returned Barty's kiss,
deepening it. Energy and heat poured from Barty, and Jim couldn't hold
back. He had been all evening, trying to make sure Barty had a good first
experience. Jim had been on simmer for what felt like hours, and holding
Barty was perfect. God, he hoped his phone stayed silent, because he did
not want to interrupt this.

Without breaking the kiss, Jim pressed Barty onto his back and into
the mattress. He tugged at the hem of Barty's T-shirt, pulling away from
his lips only long enough to get the shirt over his head.

"You have to promise me that you'll speak up if you don't like
something."

Barty nodded. "I don't know where to touch first," he whispered.
"I've… I've watched you and wondered what you'd look like out of
your clothes since I first saw you." He leaned into Jim's chest, and Jim
sat up. He straddled Barty and tugged off his own shirt so Barty could
look his fill. He stilled as Barty ran his hands over his chest and down
his belly. Jim closed his eyes and soaked in Barty's explorations. It had
been too long since he'd been touched in an intimate way, and he hadn't
known how much he missed it until Barty reawakened some deep part of
himself with the tenderest of caresses.

"Take your time," Jim whispered into the darkness, shaking
slightly. Barty sat up, and Jim held him around the waist. Lips, hot and

wet, touched his chest and then encircled a nipple. "Damn." He lolled his head back as Barty trailed his soft hands over him.

"Is that okay?"

"Honey, if you do something I don't like, I'll tell you, but if you keep that up, things are going to be over really fast." He felt like a teenager again. This was new for Barty, and in a way, that newness seemed to be heightening things for Jim as well. He smoothed his hands down Barty's shoulders, opening his eyes. Barty was beautiful. Not in the conventional way, but he was unique, and there was strength and fortitude in him that Jim thought very appealing. There was something to be said for someone who understood his lot in life and made the most of it. That was Barty in spades.

Jim brought his hands up along Barty's neck and then to his cheeks, guiding them back into a kiss. He loved touching Barty. There was something unusual about it, like he was meant to touch Barty, hold him. They fit in a way he didn't with Garrett, but he had no idea why. Jim guided Barty back down onto the bed, sliding his lips down Barty's neck to his shoulder. He licked and sucked. There was probably going to be a mark; hell, Jim hoped so. He liked the idea of seeing something of his on Barty.

"Don't...," Barty said. "What will everyone say if I go to class with a hickey?"

Jim paused. "They'll think that their professor, a very quiet and learned man, got himself some action." He leaned forward once again. "You taste like the sweetest chocolate ambrosia." He inhaled deeply, letting Barty's scent fill his nose. God, this... Barty, had been worth waiting for.

"Jim... oh God...." Barty's words trailed into a groan. "Don't stop."

"I have no intention of doing anything of the sort." He licked a path down Barty's chest, teasing each of his nipples until Barty whimpered and quietly pleaded for more. "What do you want?"

"I don't know...," Barty answered plaintively. "This is so new."

Jim understood. "But you have to have dreamed of something. When you watched the films, what did you like most?" Jim had a pretty good idea, and he slowly slid downward until his face was even with the waistband of Barty's boxers. He waited for an answer, but

Barty seemed to have stopped breathing. Jim tugged them down until Barty's cock bounced free. He licked up the shaft and then ran his lips up and down it, Barty quaking like new leaves in a spring breeze. "Is this it?"

"Uh-huh," Barty answered.

Jim slid his hands up Barty's chest and then back down to his cock, holding it and then stroking slowly as Barty moaned softly. Jim wasn't about to tease him. Moments like this got blown up in people's mind. They were dreamed of, and Jim wanted to make sure that Barty's dreams all came true and more.

"God, Jim," Barty groaned, drawing out the words as Jim slid his lips down him.

Jim remembered how that felt for the first time. Hell, each and every time it was amazing, but to have the wet heat of a mouth surround you for the first time was a sublime experience—at least it had been for him—he wanted to make sure Barty's was even better.

"Yeah. That's what I liked."

Jim hummed softly and took nearly all of Barty's considerable length. Barty was no small man, and Jim couldn't help wondering what his long, heavy shaft would feel like as it slid deep into him. Jim liked giving and getting, and it sometimes depended on the mood he was in, but at the moment, he wouldn't have minded being on the receiving end. However, that was for another day. Right now, he wanted to drive Barty out of his mind, and judging by the gasps, moans, and the way he tapped his feet on the bed, Jim was doing just that.

"Jim," Barty warned, and he backed away, letting Barty slip from between his lips. "I was so close."

"I know, but I don't want it to be over yet." Jim climbed off the bed and shed his boxers. He also divested Barty of the last of his clothes. Then he went to the far side of the room and turned on a dim light on his dresser, just enough for them to see.

Barty pulled up the covers as Jim approached.

"Why did you do that?"

"Because I'm a skinny beanpole," Barty said.

Jim tugged the covers away. "You're a stunning man, and don't let anyone ever tell you any different." He climbed back on the bed, locking his gaze with Barty's. He wanted him to know that he wasn't going to accept any argument on that point. In his eyes, Barty was damn near perfect, and he wouldn't change a thing.

"You're the one who's at the top of the stunning scale." Barty grinned as he ran his hands over Jim's arms. Jim flexed for him, and Barty hummed as he leaned in. "That's what I wanted to see."

"I feel a little silly," Jim said, relaxing his arm and pressing Barty back on the bed. That was way too close to cheesy muscle porn, and he wanted more than that. Jim rolled them until Barty was on top, gazing down on him. Jim put his hands behind his head. "I'm all yours, honey."

Barty raked his gaze over him hard enough that Jim swore he could feel it. "I'm like a kid in a candy store." Barty seemed intent on taking his time. He licked and touched Jim much the same way as Jim had Barty. He was following Jim's lead, and that was fine.

"Do whatever you think would feel good to you." Jim waited to see how Barty would react. He expected tentative and slow, but what he got was an unleashed tiger with a ton of energy. Barty vibrated with it. Everywhere he touched seemed to come alive. And after a few minutes of Barty's incredible ministrations, Jim was very near the edge. He tugged Barty down on top of him, held him tight, and they moved their hips in unison, cocks sliding past each other. Testosterone filled the air in the room. Jim brought Barty's lips to his. He needed the connection between them and wanted to try to communicate that this was more than just sex. Words weren't going to work at a moment like this, so he had to put his tongue to a better use.

"Jim." Barty whimpered and shook. He knew Barty was close to release and was most likely trying to hold off. Jim was right there as well and pressed his hands to Barty's butt, pushing them closer together, increasing the friction just enough to send Barty over the edge with a soft whimpery cry. Jim followed right behind him, holding Barty through the throes of his release, and then didn't move for quite a while.

He held Barty, letting him know that everything was okay and it was all right not to try to move.

"Is it always like that?"

"Maybe," Jim teased. "What was it like?"

"My head feels like it exploded and came back together in a happy way."

"Then that's exactly how it's supposed to feel." Jim took a deep breath and released it, continuing to hug Barty closely. "Just relax and enjoy the afterglow." His eyes were already feeling heavier than they had in quite a while, and Jim had little doubt that he was going to sleep like a baby.

"Okay." Barty rested his head on Jim's shoulder and stayed there for a long time. Eventually, Jim settled Barty back on the bed and went to get a cloth. After a quick cleanup, he turned out the light, made sure the alarm was set, and got back into bed.

Holding Barty was one of life's amazing experiences for him. Jim's mind was clear for the time being, free of shooters and bullets. He could relax and rest. Jim had little doubt that he was going to need whatever quiet and comfort he could get, because tomorrow he was sure that his investigation was going to lead him into an area he wasn't sure he was ready to go. These things usually came to a head, and Jim had learned it could happen on a dime. He hoped that moment was approaching. They had more evidence than they had ever had at any of the scenes before, and it had to lead them to something. But what?

The shooter had most likely chosen his sister's party because of opportunity. But how did he know about it unless he was already there? That was the question that rattled in his head, even as he drifted into the quiet of sleep. *Let it go.* He had a few more hours alone with Barty, and that was enough for now.

# CHAPTER 6

BARTY COULDN'T help smiling even though he knew he should keep his mind on his work. Thankfully he just had classes on Tuesday and Wednesday this term, but he still called his department head and explained some of what was going on. Barty didn't say anything about being shot at. That was something he wasn't ready to talk about, except with Jim or maybe Nicole. At the moment he didn't want his supervisor analyzing him, and Barty knew he would. After all, he was a leading expert in clinical psychology.

"That sounds like an amazing research opportunity."

"It is."

"If you need me to, send over your lecture notes and I can deliver the lecture. What you're doing is important."

"Well, the thing is that there's the possibility the shooter has turned his attention to me. So I'm staying with one of the officers for extra protection. I'll try to get into the city, but I doubt anyone here is going to let me travel anywhere alone." He looked over at Jim, who gave him a thumbs-up and a very serious, protective look. "I'll send over the material just in case. That way you'll have time to review it, but it's a seminar and they are well on their way into their projects, so it's partly checking on their progress and making time to review their questions." The lecture he was planning was on the psychosis surrounding the University of Texas bell tower shooter, but that was hitting a little close to home, so maybe Dr. Nelson would be best to present the material and lead the discussion.

"Just send it over, and I'll be prepared."

"Thank you." Barty hung up and stayed in the conference room, watching as Captain Westin and Jim had a hushed conversation. Within seconds Jim grew pale and then white as a sheet. He did regain his composure, but something was definitely wrong. Barty stood and was about to find out what was going on when Captain Westin and Jim walked over to the conference room and came inside.

"We may have a break in the case. But I'd like your thoughts on this," Captain Westin said as Jim sat. "We have closely analyzed the trajectory of the shots fired yesterday and have come to some conclusions. Jim has said that you believed one of the shots to have been directed at you, and the evidence bears that out. However, the other shot...." He glanced at Jim. "We believe the intended target of the second shot was his niece."

"Mindy?" Barty asked, letting that information percolate through his brain. "It isn't possible for her to have done anything to anyone— she's three."

"What the captain is trying to say is that there's a possibility that the shooter was trying to hurt Deidre with that shot. But why?"

Barty gasped and tapped the side of his head. "Holy hell." He turned to Captain Westin. "This is a break. I'm assuming that the shooter is the same as the other four, and since there aren't that many shootings in New Cynwood each year, that's a good guess. Also, the shooter has been escalating, so this might be the next logical step. To get closer to the actual cause of his obsession." Barty's heart pounded as ideas and thoughts raced through his head at lightning speed. "Okay." He walked over to the whiteboard and picked up a black marker. "Let's assume that this is the same shooter."

"Okay."

"He's shot four people at a distance. One shot, one kill, and then gone. He did that four times, and then we got the first phone call. That's escalation point one. Then you bring me in, and we get another. He's a little afraid now. He has an adversary. And he leaves the second message."

"Along with a clue," Jim added quietly.

"Yes." Barty added that note. "I believe that he's an academic of some sort. Now, he's been quiet for a few days, and I bet he was biding his time. The shooter received an invitation to the party. He knew about it, and his plan formed. He could take out the source of all that's wrong in the world—your sister." Barty jotted down Deidre's name and circled it. "This is the key." He could feel it. "When he arrived at his chosen spot...."

Jim spoke up. "He realized that he only had so much time before he was noticed and that Deidre was nowhere to be seen."

"Exactly, so he looks for the next best thing. He raises the gun and takes a shot at me, and then, when I go down, he shoots at Mindy, but she's already being pulled to the ground and shielded by Lightning Reflexes here."

"In addition, he doesn't want the gun to be seen, so he stays within the hedge and the bullets are deflected just enough that the shots miss. We removed two medium-sized branches with bullet marks in them that may have helped deflect the shots," Captain Westin said. "So to a large degree, we got lucky on a few counts yesterday."

"Yeah."

"But why would he take a shot at Mindy?" Jim asked.

"Because your sister took something away from him that he wanted and cared about, so he was going to return the favor. He was going to take her daughter," Barty explained.

"That's so sick," Jim said with a shiver.

"He is sick," Barty said. "He has no feelings for other human beings, and he doesn't care what happens to them. That's pretty obvious." That's what scared Barty no end. He knew he could very easily have ended up exactly like this killer. Barty had been traveling well down that path until Nana had stepped in. Heck, he had been on that path in high school after what he'd done to Milo. He hadn't cared one bit. All that had mattered was getting some sort of revenge. Making him pay for what he'd done. "At this point, I believe that all he's interested in is getting even somehow."

"But why the other shootings?" Jim asked.

"Because his anger was focused on the world. Maybe your sister's promotion to department chair is what set him off. Like I said before, this has been brewing for a while, but one event was the last straw, and that was it."

Captain Westin turned to Jim. "We need to find out who else was up for that position."

"Mason Gardener. We met him at Deidre's party. I talked to him for a while, and then Jim and I were drawn into another conversation. I don't know where he was at the time of the shooting, but he said he had to go to another family function and wouldn't be staying long." Barty never forgot a thing.

"All right," Captain Westin said, taking charge. "Let's find out where this guy was. Did we take his statement after the shooting? Was he already gone? Did he circle back and take the shots? He's officially a suspect, so let's trace every move we possibly can." He rattled off his orders, and Jim nodded while Barty took them all in. Others might not have noticed, but Jim's usually stunningly clear eyes seemed a little clouded, like his brain was still trying to comprehend what he'd been told. "Jim, can you do this?" Captain Westin asked. "There's no shame at all in asking for help. This has hit closer to home for you than anyone expected."

"I've got it."

"Good. We'll also need to talk to him, get his story, and see if it checks out. Find out all you can, locate him, and work with Philadelphia PD if necessary to bring him in."

"Got it."

"Keep me informed," Captain Westin said and left the room.

Jim did as well, following him out and then returning with the statements from the party. "Let's start here."

Barty took them and flipped through, reading all the names. "He wasn't here."

"Those are copies. Take them with us and read them. We need to go see my sister."

Jim was already on the move, and Barty hurried to keep up, carrying the papers. He got in the car, reading as Jim drove. Most people hadn't seen anything until they heard the shots and then hit the ground or raced for the house. Barty hadn't remembered seeing anything either. All his consciousness had been on being safe and making sure Jim was as well. One thing that was apparent was how impressed with Jim's actions they all seemed to be. Many people had commented on how he remained cool, had them get inside, and took off after the shooter.

Jim was about to get out of the car but stopped. "I can't do this." He radioed in for backup. "I have to have another officer here if I'm going to question my sister. This has to be official, and it can't be me taking the lead."

They sat on the street with the windows cracked to let in fresh air until another car pulled up behind them.

"Thanks for coming, Paul. Do you know Barty?"

"Of course." He'd been one of the officers to talk to him after the shooting. Barty didn't exactly have warm fuzzies about him, but he knew Paul was good at what he did.

"Deidre isn't a suspect. But one of her colleagues is a potential suspect. I need you here as a witness because she's my sister. I want someone to be able to testify that I didn't give my sister any preferential treatment."

"Is he coming?" Paul asked, turning to Barty, and Barty nodded. He wasn't going to be left outside, waiting in the car. "Then let's go." They got out of the car and started up the walk.

"Jim, has something happened?" Deidre asked as she stepped out of the house. "It must have if you're all here." She motioned, and they all went inside. She led them into the living room. "Franklin is upstairs with the girls."

"We need to talk to you. And I want to remind you not to talk about this with the rest of the family and keep this to yourself. Did anyone leave the party shortly before the shooting?"

"I was asked that yesterday, and I don't recall."

"What about Gardener? Do you know when he left?" Jim asked, and Barty watched both of them—Jim out of concern, and Deidre for signs of evasion.

"He said good-bye about fifteen minutes before the shooting, now that I think about it." She twitched her hands nervously as they rested in her lap. "He said he had a party at his brother's and couldn't stay."

"Did he seem agitated or in a hurry?" Barty asked.

"Not that I remember," Deidre answered. "You don't think that Mason... I mean, he wanted the department head job, but I doubt...." Her voice broke, and she put her hands over her face. "He wouldn't hurt either of the girls. Last week when I brought them in for the day, he took them into his office to play while I was in a meeting. He likes them, he...." She began to shake, and Jim tried to comfort her.

"We need to know," Barty said rather firmly.

"Was that before or after the announcement?" Jim asked, and Barty saw when Deidre understood.

"Before the official announcement, but there had been rumors...."

Jim nodded and turned to Paul. "Have someone look into the brother, and we can check to see where he was and if there was indeed a party."

Paul left the room, and Barty stayed with Jim. The excitement of making progress was almost more than he could bear. It really did look like they could have a solution to this case within the next few hours. Of course, then he'd go home, and Barty had no idea if Jim would be interested in him after that. Still, he kept his attention on the fact that the case could be over and people would no longer be in danger.

"Thank you, Deidre," Jim said. "We have to go, but stay with the girls."

"Do you want to see them?" she asked, and Barty wondered if Jim could at the moment. As far as Barty knew, it was a very small group of people who knew that Mindy likely had been one of the targets, and Barty wondered if Jim would be able to see her without breaking down. Jim was strong and could be hard as nails; he'd seen it. But Barty also knew that on the inside, Jim was warm and caring.

"We'll stop by this evening when I don't have to rush off. Take care of them and keep them safe."

"Dad hired some security, and they're on their way right now. They'll stay until you catch this guy."

"Good. Call if you need anything." Jim stood, and Barty did as well. Jim bent down and kissed his sister on the cheek. They left and found Paul waiting for them outside.

"The captain said that they've located the brother. He's in Philadelphia, and they're sending officers over to check on the story. They are also working with us to locate Gardener."

The excitement between the three of them was palpable, but Barty was concerned with Jim. He'd been working this case for a while now, and it had taken a turn toward the personal and gotten close to his family. He was worried. The signs of stress were there.

"Good. I hate times like this when parts of the case are out of our control."

"Me too," Paul said. "But the entire city is on edge over this, and Philly PD doesn't want this to spill over, so the captain said they were anxious to help."

"Okay, we'll meet you back at the station," Jim said, and Barty got in the car. "When are you supposed to teach again?"

"I had a lecture planned for tomorrow, but it's covered," Barty answered as Jim pulled away from the curb and raced back to the station. When they arrived and were inside, Captain Westin motioned them into his office.

"Dead end," he said evenly. "Philadelphia is sending over the statements, but Gardener's brother confirms that he did have a party and that his brother arrived about ten minutes after our gunman opened fire. Short of taking a helicopter from your sister's to his brother's, there is no way he could have been our shooter."

Jim seemed to deflate in front of Barty's eyes. "Then we're back at square one."

"No, we aren't," Barty said. "It just means that the low-hanging fruit didn't pan out and we need to look deeper. There is something here, and your sister could have spawned jealousy or the need for revenge in someone else."

"But where do we start?" Jim asked.

"Universities are hotbeds of politics and jealousies. If someone is a superstar, then they get first shot perks and funding for their projects that others don't, so they flourish while other's projects languish or die from lack of money. Then there is the appointment to department head. Some schools elect their department heads, which leads to politics. Deidre was appointed, so that means that others were passed over. Mason was passed over, but he dealt with it and was able to move on. There could have been other people who put their names forward. Remember, our shooter thinks he's the best and that the world owes him. That doesn't have to be the case."

"So all of this could exist in our shooter's mind," Jim said.

"Most of it does. The slights and overlooks are in his mind, and they have subtle influences in the real world."

"So our shooter may have put himself forward for department head and been rejected out of hand," Jim observed, and Barty nodded. "So we need to find out everyone who put themselves forward."

"I requested that from Philadelphia, and they are getting it for us. It would be needed to build our case regardless. But it's more difficult than that. We need to dig further into Deidre and find out if there are other people who might have a grudge against her," Captain Westin said. "I'm going to put Paul...."

"No," Jim said firmly. "I need to do this."

"Jim...," Captain Westin cautioned very clearly.

"No. This is my family. Would you let someone else handle it if this happened to your sister or brother?" Jim stared, and finally Captain Westin nodded.

"But you need to have backup."

"I'll be there," Barty said. "People don't like to think that anyone could want to hurt them. Deidre is more likely to tell Jim things than she is another officer. The family has been through a lot, and Jim already promised to see his nieces tonight, so he can talk to Deidre without alarming her too much." Barty wasn't lying, but he said what he did with more confidence than he might ordinarily have had.

"Don't bullshit me," Captain Westin told him, and Barty took a single step closer.

"I'm a psychologist who agreed to help you, not one of your officers. I'm still willing to help you, but not if you speak to me that way." There was a touch of the bully in the captain. Maybe not in a bad way, but he was used to getting what he wanted. "Nor will I have my expertise or honor questioned."

Captain Westin clearly hadn't been expecting that reaction.

"I told you what I would do. After all, you're the ones who brought me in and you are the reason I'm—"

Barty was interrupted by a forceful knock on the door, and then it opened.

"There's a call coming in from the same number as the last message. It's being routed to Jim's voice mail."

The door closed, and Barty felt the tension in the room spike instantly.

"Just stay here," Captain Westin said and picked up the phone. He put it on speaker, and Jim entered his access code.

"You were lucky yesterday," the same mechanically altered voice said. "I missed both your expert and her daughter on purpose. As a warning. Things need to be made right, or the next time I won't be so forgiving." The message ended.

"That's interesting," Jim said.

"I don't buy it." Barty asked them to replay the message and listened to it again. "It's short, and he's afraid. That comes through even with the distortion. He's also lying. He can't take failure, so he has to cover it up." Barty smiled.

"He also admitted to who his targets were. That at least confirms that our suspicions were right," Jim said, and Barty nodded.

"We're on the right track."

"So what's the next move?" Captain Westin asked.

"First thing, we need to realize that the game has changed. He isn't hitting his targets. The patterns we observed are pretty much out the window now, and it isn't likely he's going to return to them. He's escalating even more, and desperation is going to follow soon. He tried and failed, so next time he'll see to it that he doesn't. So he's even more dangerous than he was before."

Barty felt cold and wanted to hide somewhere. Knowing he was the one mentioned in the message was creepy, even as he did his best to keep some distance to maintain a clear head.

"What's the object of his obsession?" Jim asked, and Barty listened to the recording again.

"Definitely Deidre. Even with the distortion, he couldn't keep the scorn from coming through when he said 'her.' And to an extent I think me. It doesn't tell us much more than that. But I think that's enough. We need to dig into her promotion and how things are doing at work."

"Get a list from her of the people she works closest with. This has to be someone she has regular contact with."

"I'll talk to her tonight," Jim agreed. "My father has already hired security for the family."

"I'd also recommend that they stay at home until we can solve this case. They're still in danger, and just because he didn't get a shot at her at the party doesn't mean he won't try again."

JIM LEFT the office with Barty following. He'd done a lot of that lately.

"Jim, you need to get some distance," Barty said once they were again alone in the conference room.

"How can I? First I pull you into this case and you get shot at, and my niece—a complete innocent—gets targeted as well. I want to rip this bastard's nuts off and feed them to him for lunch." Jim's neck muscles bulged, and he pounded the table. Barty took a step back to stay out of the way while Jim let off some steam. "You can talk about distance all you want, but it's my family being targeted. How in the hell would you feel if it was your family? But it isn't, is it?" Jim asked, and Barty remained silent.

After a few seconds, Barty turned and left the room. He stomped to the coffee area and poured himself a cup. He'd had enough of anger and resentment for now. Jim could rant all he wanted. Barty's family was still a sore spot after all these years.

He stayed away while he drank some coffee and then returned to the conference room. "Are you ready to be civil instead of snappy?"

Jim didn't answer. He leaned over the table, clutching the edges.

"Where are we going to start?" Barty asked.

"Do you think it's possible that the shooter was at the party?" Jim asked. "I think Deidre said that everyone was there except Mason. So if we can plot their movements, then maybe we can figure out who's missing."

"Okay. Then call her and get a list of the people in her department. We can try eliminating everyone we can before we see her tonight." Barty didn't get any closer, but he watched Jim's shoulders slump. "We can't do this by pulling into our shell."

"I'm not, but… I went into this to protect people, and I can't even protect my own family."

"None of them were hurt, and that's because of you and your fast thinking. So don't add guilt to this. None of what happened is your doing, so keep your head in it so we can figure this thing out." He wasn't usually very good at pep talks, but Jim seemed to get a boost, so maybe he'd done something right.

"Let me call Deidre," Jim said and left the room.

Barty sat in one of the chairs, thinking about how much things had changed for him and what was likely to happen once the shooter was caught. Jim would be assigned to new cases and go on to help make the streets safer, and Barty would return to the classroom. Even after last night, he wasn't sure what would happen between the two of them. They came from different worlds in a way. Well, he could tell himself that, but the truth was, he wasn't convinced that he was interesting enough for someone like Jim.

"I got a list from her," Jim said, and Barty jumped, deep in his own thoughts at the interruption. "There are ten members of the department including her, and we've already eliminated Mason. So that leaves eight of them. We can start with the statements and see who else can be accounted for and go from there. Look for references from two people, and we'll feel good about removing them from the list."

"Sounds good." Barty could feel they were getting close. Jim made a copy of the list, and Barty began going through the witness statements. He'd read them once so there were some people he felt he could eliminate, but he found his sources and noted who could place each person during and after the shooting. "These people were together and apparently talking to your father when the shots broke out."

"These three were together, and they all corroborate it. Granted, it would be better if it were someone else, but I doubt they would collude to protect the shooter. We can eliminate Mason and Deidre, so that leaves Amy Corrigan, Stewart Hoskins, and Daniel Foster."

"Amy is mentioned in this statement, and in her statement, she said she was in the restroom when she heard the shots. It's possible it's a lie, but why would the shooter come back to the party? So the two remaining are Stewart and Daniel. I remember Stewart—he was a bit of an ass—and I spoke briefly to Daniel at one point. So I know they were both at the party," Barty explained.

"Okay. Let's speak with both of them and see if we can find out where they were."

"Shouldn't we start with Deidre tonight? She might know when they both left," Barty asked.

"Yes, and we should see if she can corroborate anything with Amy just to be thorough. I don't want to miss anything." Jim sank into one of the chairs and began going through what they had all over again, and Barty stayed out of his way and let him do what he needed to. Every now and then Jim would look up and scan the room, stopping when he turned to Barty, and then he'd go back to what he'd been doing.

Barty didn't know what to think about it all, and he sat quietly for part of the time and then opened his laptop to try to do some of his own work.


THEY LEFT the station in the early evening and went to speak to Deidre. He and Jim had developed a specific list of information they hoped to get from her. When they arrived, both girls raced down the stairs. Meghan practically jumped into Jim's arms, and Mindy stood as if waiting her turn. Barty was surprised when she tugged at his pant leg and lifted her arms. He picked her up, and she grinned at him.

"It looks like you found a friend," Jim said when he noticed.

Barty didn't really know what to do with her, but she seemed content and eventually put her head on his shoulder for a few minutes.

"Come on, sweetheart," Deidre said and gently lifted Mindy into her arms.

"We have a few things we need to know," Jim told Deidre.

She nodded. "I should have known this was more than a social visit." There didn't seem to be any heat in her voice, but maybe disappointment. "Franklin, can you take the girls upstairs?"

"I have them," Colleen said, and both girls went with their nanny.

"I'll be up to tuck you both in," Deidre said as she stood at the bottom of the stairs. Once they were out of sight, she turned and motioned toward the living room.

Jim went inside, but Barty hung back. He was feeling out of sorts and on edge and had been for hours, but he didn't understand it. Deidre's voice pulled him out of his woolgathering.

"Ask your questions, and then I have some of my own."

"Amy Corrigan," Jim prompted as Barty joined them and sat on the edge of one of the wingback chairs.

"She's pregnant and having a tough time of it. I was surprised and pleased she came."

"I remember her," Barty said. "She kept excusing herself."

"She's at that stage where she can't stay out of the bathroom, poor thing. She isn't really showing too much yet, but she's having some issues."

Jim nodded, and Barty checked that name off their suspect list. "Did you see Daniel Foster leave the party? We are trying to place him. Barty spoke with him a little, but—"

"What's going on with this fascination with my colleagues?" Deidre asked, interrupting Jim. "I want to know why you're digging into my life."

"Because we have reason to believe that you may be the focus of our shooter's obsession and we're trying to rule it out if we can." The coldness in Jim's eyes surprised Barty, but thankfully it didn't last long. "I'm trying to help keep you, Franklin, and the girls safe, so please answer the questions."

"Daniel and his husband, Felix, were here, and I remember sitting with them for a few minutes while we all waited for the police to question us. They sat pretty much where you are now and waited."

Jim turned to Barty, who was wondering why they didn't have a statement from them. That piece of information alone raised questions, and Jim left the room.

"He really is trying to help," Barty said. "I know it's very hard to keep reliving and talking about this again and again, but we do need your help and your memory."

"Does he really think it's one of Deidre's colleagues?" Franklin asked, coming into the room.

"It's possible. We've...." Barty paused. "You need to trust him. He knows what he's doing, and this is just as hard for him as it is for you. If

Jim could spare you all this, he would." He turned when Jim came back into the room a few minutes later.

"The statements were misfiled," Jim said with relief, and what Barty figured was also a bit of embarrassment. "Thank you for placing them. It was a big help. This is the last question. Do you know when Stewart left the party? We checked, and no one took his statement. He wasn't mentioned in anyone else's statement either."

Deidre paled, and Franklin took her hand. "Stewart?" she said, her eyes and mouth hardening. "So help me God, if he did this, I will tear him apart." Hatred, pure and violent, bloomed in Deidre. Barty saw it.

"Calm down, sis," Jim said. "We don't know it was him."

"He's the last one on your list, right?" She growled like a mother bear protecting her young.

"We're trying to investigate," Barty said levelly to diffuse the anger. "Why the reaction?" he asked, trying to return the focus to Deidre. "You pounced on his name and barely reacted to the others."

"Stewart is useless, and I've been working with the administration to review his performance. He doesn't teach well, his student reviews are deplorable, and his research is nonexistent."

"So you're in the process of having him terminated? Is he tenured?" Barty asked.

"Yes, he was granted tenure by a flawed committee of his cronies four years ago. I was the holdout vote on the committee, and I wrote a dissenting report that nearly scuttled the entire thing. Of course, it went through, but now his cronies are out of favor and keeping their heads down."

"So you're out to get rid of him and he knows it?" Jim asked. "How long has this process been going on?"

"The previous department head started it before he retired, and Stewart figured that with the change in management, the whole thing would die, but I've been pushing it harder, so he's angry and scared. But he doesn't do anything differently. If he'd take his work to heart, he could be a fine educator, but he's lazy and thinks the world owes him something."

Jim and Barty exchanged quick looks. "Is he a smart man?" Barty asked.

"Some might say brilliant, but he won't do anything he doesn't have to. The thing is that Stewart could be a superstar if he'd actually work at it. Some of his theories are insightful, but he wants to put them out there and let others prove them or do the work to support them. Then he wants to take the credit, and that doesn't work."

"So he left before the shooting?" Jim asked.

"He didn't say good-bye or anything, but that was the last I saw him. He wasn't exactly a popular person at the party. He has the personality of a porcupine, and yet he envisions himself as a ladies' man. That's another problem—Stewart doesn't seem to understand the boundaries between himself and his students."

"Has he ever seemed violent?" Barty asked excitedly. "Have you seen displays of anger, or is he the kind of person who'll retreat to lick his wounds and let them fester?" It seemed they had finally found the person who fit the profile he had been building in his mind. And it seemed he'd left the party before the shooting. Stewart could very well be their man.

"I don't know him very well. But he isn't an outwardly violent kind of person that I know of. I don't spend much time around him if I can help it. Stewart isn't my favorite person."

"Why did you shiver?" Barty asked. He'd noticed the small movement.

"It's nothing," Deidre said, and Franklin nudged her shoulder, still holding her hand. The show of support and love was touching and something Barty suddenly realized was very missing from his own life.

"Just say what's going on," Franklin said. "They can't help if they don't know."

"Stewart made a pass at me a few years ago. He's slimy, and it wasn't like I was going to have anything to do with him. But ever since, he's given me the creeps. I won't be alone with him, and my assistant knows that when he comes to my office that she is to follow him inside."

"How can you have evaluation discussions?" Barty asked. "Those are usually private."

"I contact personnel and have someone there with me."

"And yet you invited him to the party?" Jim asked.

"I invited everyone, and I'll be damned if I'm going to let him think he can get the better of me. There were a lot of people around, and I didn't spend time alone with him. It's best if he thinks that things are as close to normal as possible. It isn't as though I think he's going to try anything again. I just don't want to be one-on-one with him."

Jim had been taking notes, and he slid his notebook into his pocket. "Is there anything else you want to say?"

Deidre nodded. "I'm not dumb. Something started this line of questioning, and I think I have a right to know what it is."

Barty stood and walked to where she and Franklin were sitting. He knelt down so he was on the same eye level as they were. "You may have a right, but you don't want to know. This case is ugly, and you don't need to add that ugliness to your life or your daughters' lives. Protect them from it by protecting yourselves." He turned to Jim and then back to Deidre. "Once this is over, Jim will tell you everything he can." Barty had seen how the knowledge gathered in the last few hours was weighing on Jim, and he knew it would be worse for her.

"But...."

"Trust your brother," Franklin said, and Deidre finally nodded.

"Do you need anything to eat?" she asked.

"No. There isn't time. What you told us is enough that we need to get moving. Would it be all right if Barty stayed here with you? I have work to do, and I need to know that he's safe and not alone."

"Of course," Deidre agreed.

"Jim, I'm going with you," Barty said.

"Not this time." He stood and motioned for Barty to follow him to the hall. "We're going after a potential killer. I won't put you in the line of fire. I can't." Jim stroked his cheek and then kissed him, hard, possessively. "I won't lose you or put you in danger."

"What about you?"

"It's my job, and I need to do it. Deidre has security and people in the house to protect you. I'll call as soon as I can. I promise." Jim kissed him one more time and then turned and left the house.

Barty stared after him, hoping like hell that Jim would be all right and wondering how he was going to get through the next few hours without going crazy.


"JIM THINKS Mom and Dad don't accept him," Deidre said after dinner when it was just the two of them. "They just can't worry about him day after day." She sat in the perfect living room, right across from him.

"Don't lie to me or make excuses for them," Barty said. "I saw your mom and dad at the party, remember? The chill was arctic, especially from your father."

"You don't mince words, do you?"

"Why should I?" Barty said with a shrug. "Everyone talks in code and around what they really want to say. Of course, that gives me a field of study, because if we didn't hide, there would be no need for me. But I can't abide it. Your mom and dad are nothing to me other than people Jim wishes would try to understand him. He wants something they'll never give, and I doubt he realizes how badly he wants that approval from them. Since they hurt him, I'll call any excuses that are made for them."

"Okay. I find it hard to worry about him every day and so do you. I can see it in your eyes." She leaned closer.

"I'm starting to understand that." He held up a single finger. "But I believe Jim is worth it."

"How can you? You've known him a week, maybe a little longer. Things don't happen that quickly."

"I'm not sure that's true. I've studied the full range of human emotion. Romeo and Juliet knew each other for but a few nights before they tumbled off their cliff of tragic love. They died for each other after a few conversations and one night of passion. Yet we read, act out, and talk about their story, and have for hundreds of years. We want to believe that love like that is possible, and therefore, because we believe it, that love becomes possible." Barty wanted to believe that more than anything. "So yes, I care about Jim because he cares for me."

"How do you know?" Deidre asked.

133

"Because I'm here. Tonight he's going to be bringing in a suspect, and he doesn't want me in harm's way."

"But how do you know it will last?"

"I don't. Any more than you do with Franklin. Only time will tell for any of us," Barty said. "You care for Jim, so I can understand you wanting to make sure I won't hurt him."

"I don't think you will. What I'm more concerned about is that he'll hurt you."

"Why?" Barty asked.

"Because being in his life has a cost. You know that."

"I do," Barty said. He was getting tired of this cat-and-mouse conversation. "Just say what you want to say and stop this. It's tiring and useless. Jim can take care of himself. He's done it for a long time now, and I know he will continue to do so."

Deidre smiled for the first time since their conversation began. "I think you may be just what my brother needs, and he may be what you need."

"Thanks, I guess." He smiled in return. "Is that a 'welcome to the family' sort of pronouncement?"

"In a way." She turned when the clock over the mantel struck eight, and Barty hoped for the millionth time in a few hours that Jim would hurry back.

# CHAPTER 7

JIM RACED into the station and right into the captain's office. He explained everything as quickly as he could, and Captain Westin had a captain with the Philadelphia PD on the line within minutes.

"We need to pick this man up and speak with him." Jim laid out his case as logically and completely as he could. Philadelphia would cooperate, but Jim knew he had to have his ducks in a row. "He is a suspect. If I send over what I have, can you get a warrant?"

"Yes. Go ahead and send it, but we won't execute it until we speak with him to make sure we have a solid case."

"Agreed," Jim said. "I'd like to be part of the team that picks him up."

"As long as we take the lead in our city, you are welcome. Get over here, and we'll leave as soon as you arrive." He hung up, and Jim was already getting ready to leave.

"Go and get this guy. If he's guilty, I want him...." There was also the implication that if he wasn't, this was not going to go down particularly well for Jim. "Make sure he's treated as gently as possible. If we are wrong, we need to make sure relationships remain strong with our brethren in the city."

Jim got the message loud and clear. "I'll do what I can—you know that." Jim hurried out of the office and down to the cars. He took a marked vehicle because it would speed him up, and headed out.

Jim drove as fast as he could without endangering anyone. He was so close to solving this case—he could feel it. His heart raced, and his senses were hyperaware. He could taste putting this case in the completed file and going on to something else. Jim's heart raced as he wondered what a solved case would bring for him.

LESS THAN an hour later, he and three other officers approached the door of the small condo where Hoskins apparently lived. The building itself

135

was older and in need of some common-area maintenance and upkeep. Jim kept his mind on the task at hand as they approached the door.

The lead officer knocked, and they waited. He banged again. "Police!"

The door opened, and they swarmed inside. The first officer held Stewart against the wall. He was dressed in a robe, his bare legs showing from the hem to the floor.

"Why are you here?" Stewart asked as an officer held him still.

"That's enough," Jim said, cutting through the noise. "He opened the door and has cooperated." He turned to Stewart. "We have some questions, and we'd like you to come with us."

"Can I dress?"

Jim looked to the officer in charge, and he sent one of the officers with him. The others followed as well, but Jim stayed where he was. "Innocent until proven guilty."

"What if he's the man you're after?" the lead officer asked firmly.

"I hope he is." But in the back of Jim's mind was always the niggle that he could have made a mistake, and he wasn't going to be the one to trample someone's rights.

"Does this have to do with the shooting at Deidre's?" Stewart asked as the officers brought him out to the living room.

"What do you know about it?" Jim asked. If he wanted to talk, Jim was going to give him a chance.

"Nothing. I left the party because I wasn't exactly welcome there. I only went because she's the new department head and I was hoping to make a decent impression."

"Can you account for your movements? Did anyone leave with you?" He was prepared for some made-up story.

"I left and stopped at the grocery store." Stewart's hands shook as he pointed to the counter in the kitchen. "I got some bread, milk, and some fruit. The receipt is…." He tried to move, but the officers stopped him.

Jim went to the counter and found a small stack. There was one right on top from the day before, and he looked it over. It was from a grocery store five miles or so from Deidre's house, and the time was roughly the same as the shooting. This was not looking good. Now, it was possible that Stewart had found the receipt and.... Jim glanced to the bottom.

"Do you have the credit card you used?" Jim asked.

"My wallet is on the coffee table."

Jim snatched it up, opened it, and reviewed the cards until he found the one used. Then he motioned to the officers, and they released him. "I'm sorry, sir." Jim hated that they—that *he'd* been wrong.

Stewart relaxed a little, slowly approached Jim, and took back his wallet and the receipt. He put them both away. "You could have just asked if I'd seen anything...." He glared at the officers as they left the condo.

"I'm sorry we disturbed you." At times like these, Jim found that being honest and forthright helped negate some of the shock. "You seemed to have been somewhere else at the time."

"Yes, I was, and don't bother asking me if I saw anything as I left because I didn't. Not that I want to be particularly helpful at the moment. Deidre is hell-bent on ending my career, and now this...." His eyes were dark, and he clenched and unclenched his fists. They had been right about one thing—Stewart was a bundle of pent-up anger and resentment. That was for certain.

"We're sorry to have disturbed you, sir," the officer in charge said, and Jim followed him out. Once the door was closed, he followed them out to the street.

"Do you really think he didn't do it? The guy had guilt written all over him if you ask me."

"He's... I'm not sure." Jim looked up toward the windows and shook his head. "There's something about him all right, but we'll check out the alibi to confirm it. I'm sorry to have bothered all of you."

"It's happened to each of us at one point or another. He may have gotten a fright, but he wasn't harmed in any way and we didn't break anything, so he may try to raise a fuss, but it isn't going to go anywhere."

Jim rode back to the station and then drove toward New Cynwood, making phone calls as he went.

"It wasn't him?" Captain Westin asked once Jim broke the news. "We'll run down the alibi to be sure."

"Yeah." Jim was dog-tired and damn frustrated. All that work and he was right back at square one. This had been their best lead, and it hadn't worked out. "In the morning, we'll have to go over everything once again. There has to be something we missed." But at the moment, Jim could barely think straight, and he was starting to second-guess his own judgment. Maybe it was time for him to step back and turn this whole thing over to someone else.

"Let's put our heads together in the morning. Go get some rest."

Jim agreed and hung up the phone. He dropped the squad car at the station, got his own, and returned to Deidre's, where he picked up Barty and then went back to his house.

"Was it him?" Barty asked, and Jim turned. "I guess not."

"Nope. He was in a grocery store at the time of the shooting." His phone rang, and he answered it, listening as Captain Westin explained that the alibi did indeed check out. Jim thanked him and wondered what in the hell he was going to do now. He was running out of ideas, and waiting for yet another shooting was not acceptable.

ALL JIM wanted was to hide. This happened on cases sometimes. They weren't all easily solved, but this case... it was getting the better of him, and that kicked his ego right in the nads. He made sure the alarm was set and figured he'd go to bed.

"Did you eat anything at all?" Barty asked, but Jim wasn't hungry. Barty went to the refrigerator, opened it, and began pulling things out. Before Jim could say much, Barty was making sandwiches and pressed a plate in his hands. "Eat. I know this case is kicking your butt right now, but something will happen." Penelope jumped into Jim's lap, and he set her on the floor, where she prowled for dropped crumbs.

"Like another shooting." Jim sat at the kitchen island and ate absently. As soon as the food hit his stomach, he was ravenous and finished it off without thinking. "I can't let that happen."

"Then we'll look at things again and figure it out. This is only a setback, and I know you. He wasn't guilty, and you'd never want to punish someone for something they didn't do."

Jim sighed. "This guy is way too clever."

Barty sat next to him. "And he knows it."

Jim turned to him. "What do you mean?"

"Clever people often rely on cleverness. It becomes something they're proud of, just like supersmart people tend to rely on that rather than common sense. So tomorrow we'll look for the signs of his cleverness. Just like the bullet casing for redirection, the signs are there. We just have to look for them." Barty placed his hand on Jim's shoulder. "Sometimes the simplest way is the best way. But our shooter isn't going to go for that. He wants demonstrations of his superior intellect. So...."

"You think he's done the redirection thing already?"

"I think he made sure Stewart had left the party before he took his shots. Maybe the shooter knew Stewart harbored resentment against Deidre, and if Stewart had gone straight home, then he wouldn't have had an alibi and you might have arrested him and taken things further. Instead, you know who it isn't now." Barty rubbed gently. "Finish your glass of water and let's go to bed." Barty waited until Jim emptied the glass and then put the dishes in the sink.

"What's the big deal with the water?" Jim asked as Barty was finishing the dishes.

Barty turned off the water and spun around, heat building in his eyes. "I don't want you to get dehydrated." He came around the island, took Jim's hand, and led him up the stairs and down to his bedroom.

"After the day I had...," Jim began, but Barty pressed him into the room. Penelope tried to follow, but he closed the door before she could slip by.

"Last night you made me forget my own name, and now it's my turn to try to return the favor." Barty closed the door. Water or not, Jim's mouth went as dry as the desert as soon as Barty slipped off his shirt. "Is it working?"

Jim nodded, his eyes glued to Barty's slim waist as he gyrated his hips slightly. It was uncoordinated as hell and completely amazing. Jim grinned and reached for Barty. He'd begun opening his pants, and they chose that second to fall. When he tugged him closer, Barty fell right into his arms.

"That wasn't what I had planned," Barty said, struggling to stand, but his clothes had other ideas. Jim helped him to the bed and got Barty's shoes and then his pants off. "So much for smooth."

"Honey, you are beautiful," Jim said, ignoring Barty's words and trailing his hands up Barty's smooth chest as he came back to his feet.

"I'm not very good at this sort of thing." Barty swallowed hard. "I wanted to treat you to something special to make you forget, and instead I fell on you."

Jim took Barty in his arms. "You can fall against me any time you want." He brought his lips to Barty's, kissing him hard. Barty had said that he wanted to help Jim forget, and it was already working. Having Barty with him was like a balm for his spirit.

Barty worked the buttons of Jim's shirt, then removed it so their chests touched. Jim loved the feeling of Barty's skin against his, and he ran his hands down Barty's back to cup his boxers-covered butt. Firm cheeks shifted under his hands, and he clenched his fingers, kneading the flesh as he pressed even closer. He wanted more and wished he'd taken the time to remove his own pants. Barty seemed to have the same thought and began unbuckling Jim's belt. His hands shook, so Jim put his hands on top of Barty's to still them. Barty lifted his head, their gazes met, and Jim was lost. Barty's incredible eyes were a window into his deepest thoughts, and what Jim saw startled him. He'd been afraid of what he'd begun to feel for Barty, but right in front of him, in Barty's eyes, was the reflection of his own care and worries, mirrored right back at him.

Jim touched Barty's chin and kissed him as his pants slipped down his legs. Jim carefully guided Barty to the bed and then took care of his remaining clothing, stripped Barty of the last of his covering, and climbed into bed next to him.

"I want to make you forget and let you be free for a little while, but I...."

"Honey, just having you here takes away some of the worry." Regardless of what happened at work or outside the walls of his house, having Barty there in his bed felt right. Hell, it was perfect. He wasn't ready to completely give away his heart... not quite yet. But none of his other boyfriends had ever been able to settle the turmoil and sometimes unsettling ache that his job created. He spent his days seeing the worst of man's treatment of others. He needed to come home to a place where that couldn't intrude, and Barty seemed to give him that.

"That's good." Barty pulled him into another kiss and then pushed him back and down onto the bed. "Now you're mine."

"Okay. What are you going to do with me?" Jim asked, and Barty paused like he'd never contemplated anything beyond this point. It was cute and adorable. Part of Barty's appeal was his innocence and the look of delight when he found something new.

"I watched movies and stuff...," Barty said. "And I know what you did to me that I liked."

"Honey, there isn't a test, and no one, least of all me, is going to be critical or judgmental. It's all about what makes us feel good, and nothing else matters." He smiled as Barty climbed on top of him. "I know you didn't have a lot of it growing up, but think of it as playing for adults. It's about showing how you feel and having fun."

"But it's sex, it's serious, and...."

Jim pulled Barty down, stroking his back and then grabbing his ass. "It can be intense, enthralling, passionate, exciting, sublime, and many other things, but sex between people who care for each other should never be serious. That makes it sound like something that must be done, like closing a business deal, rather than engaging your heart." Jim was starting to understand just what effect on Barty's life his childhood had had on him. "Let go of what you think you must do... and just do what you want."

"But what if I hurt you?"

"If you're thinking of your partner and what they want, then you won't hurt them." He had never considered this. "Just relax, think a lot less, and be happy." Jim lifted Barty's head and cupped his cheeks. "When you took my hand, you said you wanted to make me forget about today, so do that." He wrapped his legs around Barty's waist.

"Why don't you show me?" Barty said, and Jim shook his head as he watched Barty's eyes.

"Just follow your heart. Let it guide you instead of your head." Jim got the idea that even though they were naked and Barty had planned on having sex, this had turned into something much more. He kissed him, tugging on Barty's lips, licking them lightly. "I want you to be happy. That's what matters."

"But what about you?"

"If you're happy, then I'll be happy." As far as Jim was concerned, that was how things should work in a relationship. It hadn't been that way up until then for him, but that was what he'd always hoped to find. "You're an incredible man." Jim rolled them on the bed and licked over one of Barty's pink nipples, feeling the quiver that ran through him.

"I'm skinny and…."

Jim kissed away the rest of Barty's protest. "I love the way you react to me." He figured a little exploring was in order. He kissed down one of Barty's sides, measuring the groans and gasps as he went, especially when he found that little divot above his hip.

Barty giggled and tried to pull away. "I hate tickling."

"Maybe, but I was only playing." He licked again, and Barty quivered once more. This time he didn't laugh, and his cock jerked off his belly.

"The kids used to tickle me until I threw up," Barty explained.

"I'll never do that." Jim stopped and sucked the head of Barty's cock between his lips. He didn't want to talk about what others used to do. All he wanted was for Barty to know happiness. He took more of him, listening as Barty groaned loudly while he slipped his lips down. Once Barty had closed his eyes and his mouth hung open, Jim pulled away and let him slip from between his lips.

"Why'd you stop?"

"Because I want you to be able to enjoy making love, not think it's some sublime experience. It can be that, but it's so much more." Jim settled between Barty's legs, his face right above his belly. He sucked at Barty's navel, swirling his tongue in it, stroking Barty's chest.

"But sex is important. All the books and texts say so. It's how people bond with each other."

"Yes. But it's through play, foreplay, that we really bond and get to know each other. I learn what you like, and you do the same. It isn't just insert and thrust. Sex is much more." Jim stroked down Barty's sides. "See, I'm not touching anywhere near your cock, and yet I can tell I'm driving you crazy. I do it because I want to make you happy." Jim kissed him, and Barty returned it with what felt like years of pent-up confusion and frustration.

Barty rolled them on the bed and pressed Jim's arms over his head. "I think I want to try to play."

His smile touched Jim deep down. He knew this concept was relatively new for Barty, who kissed him and then sucked on a nipple, running his fingers up and down Jim's sides. Luckily he wasn't particularly ticklish, but he still squirmed and smiled against Barty's lips.

"I like it when you play," Jim whispered.

"I don't know if I'm doing it right."

"You can't do it wrong." Jim groaned as Barty gripped his cock, stroking slowly. "Oh damn. Okay, maybe someone can do it wrong, but you can do it like that anytime you want." Jim bit his lower lip. That was heavenly. Barty tightened his grip, tugging a little faster, and Jim closed his eyes. "Don't stop."

"I won't." Barty kissed him, stroking and pressing to him. "There were all kinds of things that the guys did in those movies."

"What did you like, besides oral sex? We already know you really get a bang out of that."

"I want you inside me. But I'm not sure if it will hurt." The concerned fascination in Barty's eyes was all Jim needed to see before he knew what to do.

"How about if we leave that for a little later?" There were so many things for Barty to experience. Jim flipped them, slunk lower until his face was at just the right place, and then tipped Barty's cock upward before taking him to the root. Barty gasped, and Jim slid his tongue along the shaft while Barty moaned and whimpered. No song he'd ever heard filled him with such joy as the one Barty was singing right then.

"Jim...," Barty cried, most likely as a warning, but Jim wasn't going to stop. He sucked harder, bobbing his head until Barty's release struck both of them like a bell. Jim swallowed what Barty offered, partaking of him until Barty lay still and quiet on the sheets.

Jim let Barty slip from his lips and brought their mouths together. "That's what we taste like, you and I," Jim whispered, and Barty held him still, deepening the kiss.

Barty pushed Jim onto his back while they kissed. He had no idea what Barty had in mind, but he settled that wonder when Barty mirrored Jim's actions, kissing and licking his way down Jim's ever more sensitive body. Each touch of Barty's tongue seemed to stoke the fire within him to greater heights. His nipples ached from where Barty sucked them, and his stomach muscles fluttered at Barty's touch. He wanted more so badly, and when Barty took him into his mouth, Jim gasped in surprise and sensual anguish.

The bedding cradled him as Barty slid his lips down his shaft. He was warm and surrounded by comfort and intensity all at the same time. Jim corralled the urge to thrust his hips, pressing them down into the mattress instead so he didn't ask for too much too soon. Barty was new at this, and his technique was a little uncoordinated, but he made up for his inexperience with enthusiasm, which went a long way to blowing Jim's mind.

He clenched the bedding in his fists as Barty sucked, moving his hands and head at the same time, sending tendrils of excitement through him. Jim's balls pulled to his tingling body as the release that was building came closer and closer. Jim thought of England... or anything else he could for a few seconds in a vain effort to stave off his release.

"Barty...," Jim hissed in warning.

Barty continued his amazing ministrations, wet heat surrounding him, taking, wanting, and Jim pressed his head into the pillow as the last of his control snapped and his release washed over him like a tidal wave of ecstasy.

"Was that okay?" Barty asked, cutting through the haze of residual passion.

"Uh-huh." Jim groaned, unable to move. Barty had said he wanted Jim to forget, and at the moment, his brain was almost totally fried, so

Jim figured Barty had done a great job. He tugged Barty into his arms, letting their warmth mingle once again as he lay still, pulling air into his lungs. The world outside was going to intrude eventually, but for a few minutes, Jim could let it go and just be. It was temporary but a reprieve he loved Barty for.

# CHAPTER 8

"I KNOW it's early, but we have to get going," Jim said, and Barty waved his hand in the air like he was swatting a fly. He didn't want to get up and think about shooters or murderers. The psychotics were probably smart enough to stay in bed at this hour, so why was Jim forcing him to get up. "Honey, I have work to do, and…."

"Go away," Barty groaned even as he got out of bed.

"You were the morning person, remember?" Jim said as Barty made it to the bathroom.

"I changed my mind. Sex makes me want to sleep in." Barty wanted to go back to bed and relive what they'd done the night before, but Jim was right. They had things to do and a bad guy to catch. Barty thrust off the sleep that lingered over him and forced his mind to function.

"I'll go make coffee, and you come down when you're ready." Jim kissed him on the shoulder and tweaked his butt, which only made Barty want to hole up in bed for the entire day and not enter the world of crime and punishment.

He cleaned up and dressed, then wandered down to the kitchen. Penelope wound around his legs, and Barty picked her up, petting her while she scolded him because her food dish was empty. Barty took care of that and saw Jim had a travel mug of coffee waiting for him.

"What's the first order of the day?"

"Seeing what we might have missed," Jim answered. "There has to be something or else we're at another dead end."

"We'll find something." Barty sipped his coffee. "Why don't we get the others involved?"

"What do you mean?" Jim asked.

"If we're going to review what we know, let's get the other officers involved who have been helping you. They might have some ideas or insight. I see different things than you, so maybe one of them can help too. I don't want to step on any toes or anything, but—"

"That's a good idea. You never know when some piece will fit together." Jim led the way to the car, watching the area around them. They got in, and Jim pulled down the drive and out onto the street.

"Is something wrong?" Barty asked.

"Just keep a lookout." Jim turned back toward the front of the house. "There's nothing I can put my finger on, but I feel like I'm being watched." Jim pulled to the side of the road, jumped out of the car, and took off across his lawn.

Barty wondered what the hell was going on until a figure jumped out of the bushes and Jim leaped toward it. The two of them rolled to the ground, Jim coming up on top, and then he hauled the other man to his feet. He pulled the stumbling guy closer to the car and then dropped him on the grass.

"Jim?" Barty got out and hurried around. "What are you doing here?" he asked, recognizing Willard.

"My client didn't want to give up."

"Well, they will now, or you're going to find yourself in jail, and then we'll find out who is conspiring with you to break the law." Jim seemed ready to punch the guy, not that Barty could blame him.

"She didn't believe that he was gay and wanted proof."

"Who?" Barty asked. He was getting sick of this whole thing. "We've caught you twice, so you're not a very good detective, and Jim is about ready to take you in for trespassing and maybe breaking and entering." Barty never lied, but in this case, a little exaggeration couldn't hurt.

"I haven't done anything wrong."

"We don't know that, but I'll tell you this: someone took a shot at me the other day, so following me might not be the smartest or safest thing to do. You could find yourself in the line of fire. So why don't you tell us what this is all about."

Willard blanched, and Barty thought he was going to wet himself. "I can't say her name, but one of your students has a thing for you, and…."

Barty groaned. "This is over some coed crush or something?" *He* was ready to punch the guy. "Tell your client that I don't date students, I'm gay, and that if I find out who she is, I will fail her and turn her in to the dean." He leaned closer. "Do you think you can give her the message?"

Willard nodded.

"Good." Barty got back in the car and waited for Jim to scare the guy a little more. Then another cruiser pulled up and took Willard into custody. Barty watched out the back window until Jim walked toward the car. As soon as Jim got in and closed his door, Barty burst into laughter. "I liked that game."

"And you were good at it." Jim closed his door. "I have to radio in. The captain will want to speak to him as well to make double sure he isn't involved in any of this." After doing so, he put the car in gear. "Where did you get that breaking and entering stuff?"

"I made it up. I wanted him to start thinking jail and possible big hairy cellmates. He folded like a house of cards." Barty felt pretty good. That was one issue taken care of, and now all they had to do was catch the shooter. It wasn't going to be that easy, but Barty figured they could do it.

BY THAT afternoon Barty wasn't so sure. Willard had been released as he expected with no additional information and they were fairly sure he wasn't involved. But they all agreed to keep him on the suspect list as a precaution. The happiness and moment of mirth that had started the day had worn off long ago. Jim sat in the conference room going over everything one more time and growling like a bear with a thorn in his paw, or in his butt—Barty wasn't sure and didn't care.

"Bring in the others and go over things. You need help."

"What I need is to figure out what I'm missing," Jim snapped, and Barty had had enough.

He left the conference room, where pictures had been tacked up on boards and statements were piled on the table, and went to the captain's office. "He needs help and won't ask for it."

"What do you suggest?" Captain Westin asked as he looked up from his desk.

"Get everyone who has helped in the conference room and let's see if they have ideas. This is one man, but maybe it will take a group to catch him."

"Okay. Give me ten minutes, and I'll handle Jim when he has a fit."

"Deal." Barty returned to the conference room to more growling and even a few bangs on the table until the others started coming in.

"What do we have?" Captain Westin asked when he entered. "Barty thought we should recap for everyone, and I thought it was a good idea," he said when Jim sent him a ball-shriveling, cold look.

Jim shifted his gaze and finally looked at the others. "As you all know, we had four seemingly random shootings that gave us very little to go on. We brought in Barty to try to help us, and he's developed a psychological picture of the shooter, but we don't have much physical to go on. None of the victims seemed to have anything in common, not even a physical type."

"The shooter is smart, genius-smart," Barty interrupted. "I believe from the messages we've received that he's an academic." He quieted because he'd interrupted, but Jim nodded. "I also believe that he's angry with the world. As you know, not everyone starts shooting people when they get pissed off, but this guy has. So I believe that not only is he intelligent, but he believes he is smarter and better than everyone else."

"He has a superbig ego," the same officer who'd given them a ride the other night added.

Barty didn't remember his name and leaned in to read his name badge: Tag Miller. The guy was certainly handsome, with nice eyes and a touch of stubble on his jaw. He wasn't as handsome as Jim, but Barty could see where the ladies would love him. He wasn't Barty's type. That was definitely Jim-centric.

"Exactly, and that's what's driving him. The world isn't treating him the way he thinks he should be treated, so there is something wrong with the world, and this is his way of trying to right it."

"What about the other shooting?" Tag asked.

"That's where it gets tricky. The shooter left a message taking credit, but he's changed his MO because that shooting was more personal. That's the one we're concentrating on because if it is personal, then there is more to investigate."

"Is it true the shooting happened at your sister's home?" Tag asked.

"Yes, it did. Barty was one of the targets, as was my niece, according to the message and ballistics. We got lucky because of some interference, but we won't get a second break like that," Jim explained.

"Deidre was recently named the head of economics at Templeton. We thought that could be the incident that pushed the shooter over the edge, but the people most likely to be involved have alibis."

"Can we go over them again?" Tag asked. "I know I checked out some of them."

"All right." Jim wrote the names of all Deidre's colleagues on the whiteboard. "These five were at the party, and we have statements from them afterward with corroboration. I don't believe the shooter would have time to take the shots, hide the weapon, and rejoin the partygoers inside the house, but we also took the fact that others remembered them in their statements as further backup. So these three are off the list, all right?" Jim asked, and heads in the room nodded. "Stewart we paid a visit to. He was at a store and has a time-stamped receipt, and a cashier remembered him. So he wasn't around at the time of the shooting either. Amy was in the bathroom. She's pregnant, and wasn't feeling well at the time of the shooting."

"I remember her," Captain Westin said. "I took her statement, and she asked to excuse herself to go to the bathroom again. She grumbled that she'd been living in bathrooms lately. Poor lady."

"Okay. That leaves Mason Gardener. We thought of him at first," Jim said. "But he said he had another party and couldn't stay. Deidre said he left fifteen minutes before the shooting."

"I was assigned to check it out and went to the brother's house." Tag pulled out his notebook. "A Rodney Gardener. He answered the door, and I confirmed his identity."

"How?"

"I asked him," Tag said, as though it were the most natural thing in the world. "The place looked as though there had been a party and was being cleaned up. There were a few bottles and cups on the coffee table. I took his date of birth and all that and asked him about his brother. He said that he'd been there and had left an hour before."

"Did he seem surprised to see you?" Barty asked, and Tag turned to him, blinking.

"No. He asked why I was there, but there wasn't any nervousness or wonder about what was going on. He answered my questions, and that was it."

"What are you thinking?" Jim asked, and Barty's heart began beating a little faster.

"People are always nervous when it comes to the police. They wonder if they've done something wrong or if someone they love is hurt. But they don't just answer the door and offer an alibi as though it's an everyday occurrence... unless they're expecting it."

The tension and anticipation in the room went through the roof.

"So do you think he was covering for his brother?" Tag asked. "Like I said, he didn't seem nervous or like he was lying. He said the kids were in bed and he was talking quietly, but that seemed normal enough."

Barty turned to Jim. "Do you have pictures?" Jim handed him one, and Barty passed it to Tag.

"That's Rodney," he said confidently. "He was wearing different glasses, but that's the guy who answered the door."

"That's Mason," Jim said, and Barty turned to Jim, half in shock. "Oh my God."

"Pick up Mason Gardener right the hell now. Jesus, this guy has balls of steel. And find out where Rodney is and bring him in as well." Captain Westin looked at Tag, and Jim was already gathering his things.

"Let's go. I have Mason's address. We can get him and then pick up his brother." Jim practically ran out of the conference room.

"Be careful," Barty cautioned. "Mason isn't going to go down without a fight."

Jim paused at the doorway, letting the others through. "Why?"

"His ego. He's better and smarter than everyone. He's also a damn good shot. Take plenty of backup. He's shot four people and took a shot at two others. He doesn't care who he hurts as long as he gets what he wants."

"Okay," Jim said. "I have to get ready to go."

"I'm already requesting a warrant. We'll work with Philadelphia to get it executed, but we have to do this right. They're still smarting from yesterday. But this has to be the guy."

"I'd say we have him this time. Posing as his brother clinches it," Barty said. "Just be careful and wear the vest." He didn't want to imagine what could happen to Jim. More than once he'd worried about what Jim was going through. It had been hard last night, but this was even worse. He knew Jim was walking into a potential firefight.

Barty watched Jim leave and then hunkered down in the conference room, surrounded by the documentation of the case they had been working on and wondering what the hell was going to happen. He thought about trying to work, but there was nothing he could do. His mind wasn't going to settle on anything other than the danger that Jim was going to be in.

"How does your wife do it?" Barty asked as Captain Westin walked in the room.

"I've been married twice, and my first wife couldn't take it after a while. She said that all she did was worry from the time I left for work until I got home. Eventually she left, took our daughter, and moved to a different part of the state. I see Carolyn on weekends when I don't work and for a few weeks during the summer when I take vacation. My second wife has refused to have children. She's strong, but she won't put kids through this, and I don't blame her. This job is hard on families."

Barty nodded. He could understand that.

"But—" Captain Westin sat in the chair next to him. "—police officers are loyal to each other and I like to think they're loyal to the ones they love. I will do anything for my daughter and my ex-wife. So I know this is hard, and the waiting is the worst, but remember that the job he's doing is to keep everyone safe. It's part of his nature and what makes him good at his job."

Barty didn't doubt that. What he was questioning was himself. Was he going to be able to take it, or was he going to end up feeling like the captain's ex-wife?


HE SAT for the next couple of hours, pacing, sitting, standing, and pacing again. Finally he heard the clamor as Jim and the officers returned. Anger and frustration filled the station.

"He wasn't there," Jim said. "His house looked like he hadn't been there in a few days, probably since the shooting on Sunday, maybe longer."

"Are you looking for him?"

"Yes. We have APBs out for him and his cars. He isn't going to get very far. Look, I called Deidre, and she's hunkered down at her place. I'm going to have an officer take you over there. You'll be safe, and you won't have to sit here. I have hours of work to do, and you don't need to wait around for me."

"I'm fine, Jim," Barty said firmly and sat back down. He didn't want to be sloughed off. "If you want to shove me off somewhere, just say so."

Jim closed the door. "What? I want you to be safe, and the rest of the day is going to be pretty dull. You were a great help in so many ways. But...."

"Like I said, if you're done with me and don't want me around any longer, then just tell me." Barty knew when he was being dismissed. He'd done his part. Jim had solved his case, and all he had to do now was find the bad guy. Everything else was going to be wrapped up.

"Of course you can stay if you want." Jim sat in the chair next to his. "I only thought you'd be more comfortable at Deidre's than here."

"Why would I be more comfortable at your sister's than here with you? That doesn't make much sense to me unless you want me out of the way, and if that's what you want, I'll get Penelope and go back to my apartment. It isn't likely he's going to show up there now that the entire police force is on the lookout for him."

"Is that what you think?"

"I really don't know. At some point self-preservation takes over for all of us, and if he's figured out that his plans are up in smoke, he'd have a plan to get the hell out of Dodge. Once the facts are known, it doesn't make sense for him to be anywhere near the source of that knowledge. If it were me, I'd either get out of the country or go to the West Coast or somewhere I could blend in and figure out what to do. Grab a car and start driving. But then, who knows? In times of stress, people will do the most unexpected things." Barty lifted his gaze to Jim's. "Like spend time with someone like me."

"Jim," Tag said as he opened the door and stuck his head in.

"I'll be right there," Jim answered, and Tag closed the door. Jim turned back to face Barty. "This case has been the most difficult of my career. People have died, and members of my family were shot at, but meeting you has been the one bright spot in this whole thing." He smiled. "I have to go, but like I said, if you don't want to sit around here and wait, I can have someone drive you to Deidre's."

Barty swallowed hard. "I'm fine." He did his best to sound reassuring, and Jim left the room.

One of the officers came in and began gathering up the papers and files so they could be taken care of properly, so Barty got out his computer and went to work as best he could while minutes stretched into hours.

"LET'S GO home," Jim said about the time Barty was ready to put his head on the table. He couldn't keep his eyes open any longer.

Barty nodded, gathered up his things, and followed Jim out to the car. They drove home with him dozing in the seat. "No luck?" he asked when they neared the house.

"No. Everyone is still looking. We'll find him. It's hard for people to completely disappear. There are too many ways that we all make contact with each other. Social media, credit cards, financial transactions… we're watching them all." Jim pulled up the drive, opened the garage door, pulled in, and waited for it to close. They got out of the car, and Jim went inside, deactivating the alarm.

Jim trudged tiredly ahead of him, and Barty turned to close the door. "Do you need something to eat?" he asked, looking over his shoulder at Jim.

He never heard Jim's answer. Pain bloomed on the back of his head and everything went black.

# CHAPTER 9

JIM STARED at Mason Gardener in his own home and wanted to tear him limb from limb. Barty lay unmoving on the floor, and Jim tried to keep his attention on the man pointing the gun at him and not on Barty's prone form. At least he didn't see any blood.

"So this time we meet under very different circumstances," Mason said. "This time I don't have to make nice with your brownnosing sister at her sickening party. God, I nearly got sick a dozen times. That bitch celebrating her promotion, the one that should have been mine. My work is far superior to hers, and much more insightful. I developed theories and practices that are used all the time, and she did nothing but plod along on work that will never get her anywhere."

Jim knew he had to keep Mason talking so he could think of something to do.

"Take out the gun from under your jacket slowly and put it on the floor," Mason said, and Jim complied, kicking it off to the side before taking a step away from Barty and Mason. "That's better. Things would be perfect if it was your fucking sister here, but once you're out of the way, she'll get hers, and then everything will be the way it should be."

The guy was delirious, but Jim didn't say anything about that. "Why do all this? I understand about losing the chance at a job, but why take shots at people on the street?"

"They're all guilty. I've done incredible work, but every time I turn around, some member of the Main Line old guard was there to stop me. You think that because you have money, you can all do whatever you want. Your sister tried to bring disciplinary action, but I was able to get around her then. The administration and my true peers saw my value and stood up to her. But she stood in my way on the curriculum committee and relegated my classes to electives. And this time she was able to get what she wanted, a promotion that should have been mine." His eyelids twitched, and the hand he was holding the gun with shook a little. His pent-up rage wasn't going to be held at bay for much longer.

"I don't understand...." Jim kept his voice level and glanced at Barty, hoping he wasn't hurt too badly.

"You wouldn't. Look at this damn house. It's huge, and you expect that this kind of thing is your due. You didn't work for this house. It was given to you by Daddy or Grandpa... someone else who made the money. I didn't have that!" he yelled. "I'm smarter than you, and yet I don't get ahead. Soon all of us, the ones who get pushed aside, are going to rise up and take over. After all, we have the brains and cunning. All we need to do is get rid of the people like you or make you all so scared that you shut yourselves in your houses and let those of us better than you make the decisions."

Jim took another step back and then another.

"Stay where you are," Mason said. "Don't think I don't know what you're doing. You have some other weapon hidden somewhere. Well, that isn't going to help you. Pull out that chair and sit your useless ass down. God, you had to bring in someone like him." Mason waved his free hand absently toward where Barty still lay. "But even then you only got lucky."

"And you took some chances," Jim said.

"One has to take chances to get anywhere."

Jim didn't argue. "Why not run and try to start a life somewhere else?" What Mason was doing was stupid. The police were still going to be after him, and they weren't going to rest if he hurt one of their own. Jim was certain of that.

"Run?" Mason stepped forward. "That's what your lot do. I know I'm done. People will find out, and that's the end of me. But I will strike a blow for true justice and equality. I'll take care of you and your little friend here and then your bitch of a sister. I'm going to go out in a blaze of glory."

Jesus, this guy didn't care anymore. All he wanted was his revenge, and then he intended to decimate Jim's family and take his own life. "Barty, can you hear me?" Jim asked, hoping for some sign that he was okay.

Barty didn't move.

"Don't concern yourself with your little boyfriend there. It doesn't matter if he's dead or not. He will be shortly." Mason's eyes swirled, and Jim wondered if he was on something. Had he been drinking? Or worse, were drugs involved and the chance of reasoning with him completely out of the question?

Jim took one last step back. He was up against the wall, literally and figuratively. Mason took another step as well.

Jim had no idea what in the hell to do. No one was going to be coming to their rescue. The alarm was off, and he had no way of triggering it. Not that it would help. If he did, Mason would shoot them both and take off. There had to be something he could try. Jim was a trained police officer, and all he could think of was to talk.

"It isn't too late, you know."

Mason laughed maniacally. "Don't bullshit me. I know what I've done, and there's only one way this is going to end. You can't talk me out of it or play on my conscience or sense of empathy. I don't have one. You people are nothing, and you're lucky I haven't shot you already, but I like watching you squirm, just like I loved watching you all run in circles trying to figure things out. You couldn't do it on your own, so you had to have help. I don't need help, and I'm not weak enough to have to ask for it. I know what I want, and I'm going to get it before I end this once and for all." He waved the gun, and Jim braced for a shot, but none came. "Are you going to wet yourself?" He turned quickly to glance at Barty, but the gun didn't waver.

Jim realized that might have been his only chance, that split second, and he hadn't taken it. "What do you want me to do?" He had to try something.

"Nothing! I want you to do nothing but die. I've had it with your entire family and what they represent. So I'm going to wipe them all out. That will send a clear enough message."

Whatever the hell this guy was trying to say, Jim found he wasn't able to follow. "Why don't you tell me your message?"

Mason stepped forward, cocking the gun. "Why don't I shoot you now and get this over with?"

He moved closer, and Jim's heart pounded in his chest, the blood ringing in his ears. He knew his time was coming to an end. Jim closed his eyes and thought of Barty, wishing that they'd had more time together and he hadn't failed and been able to save him. He was out of options at this point, and he braced for the end, hoping it would be fast.

A single shot filled the room, hurting Jim's ears. He waited for the concussion of impact and then the bloom of pain, but felt neither. Jim pried his eyes open in time to see Mason crumple in front of him and Barty's hand fall back to the floor, clutching his gun.

"He really is an idiot," Barty said breathlessly.

"What the hell did you do?" Jim asked as he removed Mason's gun from his hand, checked that he didn't have another, and hurried to Barty.

"He was going to kill you, so I grabbed for the gun and shot first." Barty slowly sat up with his back resting against the cabinets. "Go ahead and call whoever you need to."

Jim ignored him and took Barty in his arms. "God, you saved me, and you're all right." He cradled Barty's head, lightly stroking his hair.

"Jim, I have a huge headache. Just call an ambulance, please, and maybe someone to take that mess away." Barty rested against him as Jim fished his phone out of his pocket.

"I need police and an ambulance." He gave his address. "Please relay that a police weapon has been discharged and that there is a suspect down. Two in need of medical attention." He hung up and called Captain Westin. "I need you at my house now. The suspect is on the kitchen floor. Barty shot him with my service revolver. Please just get here right away." Jim hung up the phone. He had no intention of checking to see if Mason was still alive or touching him in any way. He held Barty until sirens sounded outside.

"I need to go," he said, and Barty leaned back against the counter. Jim left the kitchen and opened the garage door so that help could easily get to them. Rescue workers streamed in, one starting on Mason and the other helping Barty. Captain Westin arrived at the phalanx of the police contingent, and they spoke with Barty, who was being helped onto a stretcher and getting ready to be transported.

"We think he might have a concussion, and we need to have him checked," one of the EMTs said as Barty was whisked away.

Captain Westin assigned Tag to follow him, then turned to Jim. "What happened?"

"He was here, waiting. As soon as I deactivated the alarm and we were inside, Mason knocked Barty out and held me at gunpoint. He disarmed me, and I slid my weapon as best I could toward Barty and then slowly led Gardener away. I had no idea if Barty could hear what was going on or not. He didn't show any signs of being conscious, but when Mason was about to shoot me, Barty sprang into action and shot Gardener first." Jim was still shaking. "He's a hero, Captain, without a doubt. I don't know how much he heard, but he acted just in time to save me."

"Did the suspect say anything?"

Jim nodded. "He confessed to the whole thing. He wanted to set the world to rights, in his own mind anyway. Barty was right on the entire time. Gardener was smart and thought everything should have gone his way. He intended to kill me, Barty, and then my sister and her family before probably taking his own life."

"But why shoot people on the street?"

"It seems he blamed what he called Main Line people for holding him back. So I suspect that what started as a way to get even with the world narrowed to Barty and my sister. Barty because he could have caught him, and my sister because of their history." Jim was getting antsy. He wanted to get to the hospital to see how Barty was doing, but he had a job to do here. "At least it's over. I'm sure Barty will be able to break down the psychology much better than I can, but let's just say the guy was off his nut." *To say the very least.* "He thought he was smarter than everyone else, but it was that hubris that brought him down. If he'd have backed away, it would have been nearly impossible for us to catch him."

"Probably. But it isn't likely his psychological state would ever have allowed that. As long as the source of the inequity existed, he couldn't let it go."

Jim knew Captain Westin was right, but he, Deidre, and Barty, as well as his family, had almost paid a very dear price for his craziness.

"Let's get your statement and finish up here. Then you can go to see Barty."

Jim nodded and sat down with one of the other officers, explaining in detail what he'd seen and what had happened. "Is he dead?" Jim asked Captain Westin once he was done.

"Yes. Barty got him square in the back, and it must have ripped him up good inside. It was a good shot, and it isn't likely he suffered for very long. I know that's little comfort, but it might be to Barty."

Jim remembered the first time he'd discharged his weapon at a suspect. He'd killed the man, and sometimes he still saw his face in his sleep. It didn't matter that he'd been threatening him with a gun at the scene of the crime and had the money from the robbery on his person. Ending someone's life was never to be taken lightly, and Barty had done just that to protect him.

"When the time comes, I'll tell him." Jim waited until the entire kitchen area of his home had been processed, photographed, and reviewed. Finally, after several hours, he was able to leave and went right to the hospital.


BARTY HAD been moved to a room and seemed asleep when Jim walked in. At least he only seemed asleep, as opposed to knocked out on the kitchen floor. For as long as Jim lived, he would never forget that sight. It was indelibly etched in his mind, and he was sure he'd see it in his dreams for some time to come. He didn't want to wake Barty so he stood quietly in the doorway.

"Jim," Barty said after a while, opening his eyes and turning his head on the pillow. "I could feel you looking at me."

"I didn't mean to wake you."

"If you hadn't, I'm sure a nurse would have been in to make sure I was responsive. They check every twenty minutes, I swear. That's the thing about hospitals. It's for sick people, and sleep is the best medicine, but they never let you sleep. Or at least they won't let me sleep."

"It's the concussion thing."

"They said I'll probably come home tomorrow. They want to monitor me overnight." Barty closed his eyes, and Jim walked to the bed and took his hand, a feeling of rightness and contentment washing over him. "How did it go after they took me away?"

160

"They gathered everything and will run ballistics to prove that the shooting was justified in case there are any questions, but it's nothing to worry about. He had me at gunpoint, and you're a hero."

"Is he dead?" Barty asked in a whisper.

"Yes," Jim answered.

"So I killed someone." Barty's voice was barely audible. "How do you deal with something like that?"

"You don't." Jim pulled up a chair and sat, then took Barty's hand again. "It isn't something you deal with—it's something you accept. You were only protecting me... us. What you did was right. He was going to shoot me."

"I know. I acted without thinking. I couldn't let you die. I didn't know what I'd do if you weren't around. Penelope likes you, and I think...." He trailed off, but then he picked up his thought. "I've lived alone for a long time and thought I would forever. I don't want to do that again," Barty said quietly. "I know that isn't very romantic, but I don't have good words for how I feel. This is all so new for me."

"You don't need to be flowery. Simple words are sometimes the best. Like the fact that, when I saw you on the floor, knocked out, part of me wished he'd hurt me instead of you. I wanted to tear him apart for hitting you."

"Why?"

"Because I love you." That was the simplest and most direct answer to a question that Jim could ever remember giving. It was the truth, and hiding it or beating around the bush wasn't right. He needed to say it, and Barty needed to know.

"Good." Barty closed his eyes once again. "I love you too. It's hard to know how to say something like that to another person. I mean, is it okay to just say it, or do I need to say something more involved?"

"What does your heart say?" Jim leaned closer, and Barty kissed him. The touch was light but with enough energy behind it that Jim fingered his tingling lips. "Does it need flowery words? Because I'll give you anything and everything you want."

"Nope. Just you."

"Then you have me." Jim stayed where he was, leaning over the bed, his face near Barty's. He closed the distance, rubbing his cheek

161

against Barty's, sharing his warmth. "You just have to promise that you won't run off to someplace like Boston if you get a better offer."

"Don't want to go anywhere." Barty reached up and patted Jim's head. "I'm happy here, and there's one less killer, so the city's safer."

Jim closed his eyes and let himself be content. They had a long way to go after all the excitement that brought them together, but he was more than ready for some quiet time together.

JIM WENT in early the next morning to deal with the mountain of paperwork. Barty called just before noon, and Jim took the rest of the day off. He picked Barty up from the hospital and brought him back to his home. At the house, Penelope talked to them as they came in, and followed Barty up the stairs. When Jim got him into bed, Penelope settled next to Barty and stayed there as if she knew he wasn't feeling well.

"I'm not an invalid," Barty said, trying to stifle a yawn.

"Right. You only got a few hours of sleep, so rest, and I'll be downstairs if you need anything." Jim left and got Barty some water and juice. He set the glasses next to the bed in his room before leaving and closing the door most of the way. He went back down and met the cleaning service at the door, asking them to be quiet while they worked. "No vacuuming today."

"Of course," they said, and Jim went to the family room to watch television.

Barty joined him after less than an hour, carrying Penelope in his arms. He sat next to Jim, and within half an hour, he was asleep, resting his head on Jim's shoulder. Barty hadn't said anything, but Jim had a feeling that sleeping alone wasn't something Barty was going to be comfortable with for a while. He knew the dreams would come eventually; they did often enough for him.

Jim settled Barty on the sofa and put the blanket over him. Penelope found a spot she liked, and Jim moved to the nearby chair and spent the afternoon watching the television and standing guard to keep the dreams away in case Barty needed him. Eventually Jim put his head back and closed his eyes, getting some of the rest he'd been denied for weeks.

BARTY WOKE with a start, thrashing and covering his head.

"It's all right," Jim said, lightly stroking Barty's shoulder. "It's just a dream." Penelope jumped down and raced off while Jim did his best to calm Barty. "Barty, you need to wake up."

"What?" Barty asked. He was half off the sofa, and Jim helped him to get settled again so he wouldn't fall. "He was here again.... He came back."

"It was only a dream. He's gone and he isn't coming back."

"I know." Barty relaxed on the cushions.

"I know you know about things like this, but I can have you come in and talk to someone in the department. We deal with the aftermath of shootings all the time. It might do you some good."

"You have a department psychologist?"

"Of course, and he's helped a lot of us after shootings. It's natural to be upset about it, and just because you're a psychologist yourself doesn't mean you don't need someone to talk to."

"But what is he going to tell me that I don't already know? The dreams will fade in time, and I shouldn't hold in my feelings and try to be strong. I should talk about what happened and let it process. Nothing can change the fact that I was shot at, attacked, and that he was going to kill you, so I shot the bastard first. And if I had to, I'd do it again." Barty pulled the blanket up to his chin. "Does that make me bad? Like him?"

*Oh God.* "No. Of course not."

"But I could be him if things had been different. So what if this changes me?"

"Do you want it to change you?" Jim asked, but Barty shook his head. "You are one of the most self-aware people I've ever met. You know what makes you different and why. Sometimes I think that self-awareness creeps you out, but I think it's what's saved you all this time. You were aware of who and what you are. So instead of going down Mason's path, you chose your own."

Barty nodded. "You should have been a psychologist."

"I like being a police officer, and I think one psychologist in the family is quite enough." Jim waited for Barty's reaction and got a bright smile. "See, you already know your own answers. You just have to think about it a little. Besides, I think once you've had a little distance and you have a chance to look into things, because I know you will, you'll see that you and Mason don't have as much in common as you think."

Barty rolled his eyes. "Okay, enlighten me."

"I can't because I don't have the facts, but he was consumed by hate and jealousy. I don't see those things in you. You're a gentle, caring man who needs to learn how to have a little fun." Jim looked up at the blank television.

"I don't think I can play right now, but after my head stops aching, I'll kick your butt at that driving game." Barty closed his eyes.

"You will?"

"I'm a good driver… when there aren't a whole bunch of other cars on the road."

Penelope meowed as she jumped back on the sofa and began kneading herself a bed near Barty's feet. Then she lay down, blinking at Jim like he needed to go back to his place because it was nap time. Barty seemed tired once again, and Jim left the room to let him rest.

His phone rang as he entered the kitchen. "Is it true?" Deidre asked breathlessly when he answered. "It was Mason after all?"

"Yes. He attacked Barty and me here at the house, and Barty shot him."

"I knew I never really liked him. So it's safe and I don't have to have the security any longer?"

"No. But he was obsessed with you and rattled off a list of grievances that centered on you. I'm not saying you did anything wrong, because Mason was clearly not thinking right. But I know you can drive and strive for what you want."

"Ambition isn't a bad thing."

"No. Just think about bringing the others along with you."

"So this was my fault?" Deidre snapped.

"No. It was all his fault. Mason is to blame for everything he did. He took everyday events and blew them into huge deals that threatened his self-image and ego. I doubt anything could have changed what happened. If it hadn't been you as the trigger, it would have been someone else. As you said, he was smart but not willing to do the work. That wasn't going to get him anywhere in the long run. So either you would have stood in his way, like you did, or it would have been someone else."

Deidre was quiet as Jim went upstairs and got the empty glasses from beside the bed and brought them back down to the kitchen. "So what do I do?"

"Go on with your life as best you can. It's over now. Be grateful and happy."

"So it was definitely Mason. It's unsettling to know I worked with someone capable of doing those kinds of things." She sounded much more subdued now.

Jim wasn't sure what to say that wouldn't sound trite or cliché. "The best thing to do is to face it head-on and truthfully. Be honest and let people form their own opinions. If anyone needs help because of what happened, get it for them. Were there any people particularly close to him in the department?"

"Not really. He was a loner and didn't work well with his colleagues."

"Look, I'm going to let you go. I need to watch Barty for a few more hours to make sure he's going to be okay. Tell the girls that I love them and give them each a hug for me." Jim hung up and found the cleaning ladies, who were finishing up the upstairs bathrooms. He gave them a few instructions and returned to where Barty was sleeping.

Jim ended up spending much of the rest of the afternoon reading, and he took a nap as well. He hadn't realized how tired he was or how hard he'd been working these past few weeks until he'd taken a few minutes to slow down.

"Jim...," Barty said, jerking Jim from the doze he'd been in. "I should go back to my apartment. I've been staying here because of the case, but Penelope and I should go back."

Disappointment stabbed through him. Jim had known all along that Barty would go home eventually, but now that the threat had passed, it was time for that to happen and Jim wasn't sure he wanted Barty to leave. The house was huge, and living there alone was like rattling around in a maze sometimes.

"You can do whatever you like, Barty. Is that what you want?"

"It's what I have to do. I can't keep staying here and living off you. That's not right." Barty lowered his head back onto the pillow. "I'll pack up my things and go home tomorrow morning. I don't have that much here, and I can take the train while you're at work. I need to return to my classes anyway. It's not fair to have someone else doing my work for me."

Jim didn't argue with him. He liked having Barty staying there. Not only was he less lonely, but Barty filled his time with light and made the house feel alive, something it hadn't in quite some time. There was no use fighting it, and what Barty said was logical, but it didn't necessarily make him happy.

After a while, Jim left the room to make something to eat. He needed something to do. The refrigerator was stocked, so he made some pasta and sauce for dinner, brought a plate to Barty, and turned on the television. They ate and spent much of the evening watching whatever was on until it was time for bed.

Barty had been injured, and there was no way they could do anything, but Jim was pleased when Barty joined him in his bedroom, and they both climbed under the covers. Barty settled close to him, and Jim cradled him in one arm. He should have been tired. It was late enough, and physically he was still tired, but his mind refused to shut down, so Jim spent much of the night lying awake, listening to Barty and Penelope's soft snores.

"I want you to stay here," Jim said at one point, but Barty was sound asleep. He only wished he'd had the guts to say those words when Barty had been awake to hear them. He wondered why he hadn't, and it came down to fear. His own and the fact that Barty might not be ready for a step like that. So Jim finally fell asleep, but he didn't get very much of the rest he needed.

"WHY ARE you as grumpy as a lion this morning?" Tag asked after the case follow-up meeting.

Jim wanted to make sure that all reports and statements had been gathered before they closed the case and officially put it to bed. It should have been a happy time, in a way. The threat to the community was removed and people were safe once again, but Jim had been nitpicky about more than one thing, and the others hadn't been happy about it.

"I just want this to be right," Jim answered.

"Did you and Barty have a fight or something?" Tag asked. "The whole station knows the two of you have a thing for each other. To most of us, it's no big deal. Did you think we'd be angry or something?"

"It was mixing work and my private life, so I tried to keep them separate." It wasn't like he'd hidden who he was; he just didn't talk about it.

"So I take it there is something going on." Tag pulled up a chair.

"Why the Gossipy Gertie all of a sudden? Is there some sort of pool started?"

Tag looked up to where some of the other officers were standing. "There is. So what's the deal?"

"That's what I have to find out," Tag said. "To know who wins."

Jim stood and walked to where everyone was grouped and held out his hand. Robbins placed the sheet in it, and Jim looked it over. "Hand me the money," Jim said flatly, and Robbins reached into his pocket and passed him two twenties. "This is it?" Jim asked and slipped the bills into his own pocket. "You're all wrong, so I'll put it in the coffee fund." He glared at each one. "No, I did not ask Barty to marry me and he turned me down, and no, we did not have a fight… and neither of us is pregnant. God, who was that stupid? Forget it. Don't answer, you smartasses." Jim turned and walked away to grumbles from behind him.

"I told you there wasn't some kid involved," Tag said to Robbins.

"It was the standard pool blank," Robbins said. "I didn't have time to make up a special one. So what's the real answer?"

"I'm fine. Barty is just going back to his apartment," Jim said from his desk, looking over his paperwork. "Don't you all have work to do?"

They turned and got busy while Jim finished up and was called to the scene of a break-in. It split up his day, and he was able to find the source and the culprit pretty quickly, and then returned to the station for still more paperwork. By the time he left for the day, he was exhausted. Jim stopped for dinner on his way home, then to the house and right up to his bed, which seemed way too big and definitely too empty for his liking. He sent Barty a good-night message and then turned out the light.

# CHAPTER 10

BARTY SIGHED as he sat in his office, staring out the window at the quad in the center of campus. It had taken less than an hour after his return for the details of what he'd done to sail across the entire campus. His male students suddenly thought he was the cat's meow, and his female students looked at him as though he'd hung the moon. Both situations made him nervous as hell.

"Did you really do what they say you did?" a female voice asked, and Barty turned toward the doorway. "Did you really shoot that serial killer?"

"Yes, I did. But it was out of necessity." He groaned inwardly. He didn't want to review the details of what had happened with his students. "I will have some great opportunities for research, though. I've got appointments already with his coworkers, as well as his family. So we'll see if any new information comes of it. What can I help you with?"

"Nothing really," she said, hoisting her notebook a little higher up her chest.

"Carry Ann, there is one other thing that came out of this whole episode," Barty said.

"What's that?" she asked, her eyes widening as she pushed away from the doorframe.

"I think I may have found a boyfriend." He probably should have said nothing, and she deflated like a balloon. "It's pretty awesome. But is there anything I can help you with? Your final papers are due next Friday, and I'm looking forward to reading them. So I hope you've started." Barty figured his little announcement would probably make it around campus just as quickly as the news of his serial killer encounter, and that was fine. He didn't mind what other people thought, and if it kept the girls from their interest, then it was a win. He figured he probably should have come out, as it were, a while ago. This whole thing with Willard stalking him could have been avoided completely.

"Thanks. I've already started on my paper, and it's going to be amazing. I decided to do some work on the UT shooter incident. This whole incident has me interested, and I have an appointment with one of the original researchers to talk with him tomorrow. So that should be awesome." She hurried away, and Barty returned his attention to the flowers in the courtyard.

The last two days had been... well... boring as hell. Even Penelope lazed around the apartment, and when he came home, she trotted past him looking for Jim, he was sure of it. They had talked and texted, but that was it. Jim was busy with his work, and it was nearing the end of the term, so Barty was going to be under a severe time crunch. Still, he was whiling away the time, just looking out the window instead of preparing his research materials. His mind kept going back to how he'd worried over Jim when he'd gone out to pick up Mason, and at the time, he'd wondered how he could deal with the not knowing. Now, just after a few days, he understood that the worrying over not knowing what was happening was better than being away from Jim, and going home to an empty apartment rather than a home with someone who really cared for him was a letdown. Maybe once this week was over.... Barty sighed for what seemed like the millionth time and pulled his attention back to his work.

Of course, he made no progress, and what he did write was crap. He ended up deleting it all and shutting down his computer. This whole thing had him at loose ends. He hadn't really wanted to go back to his apartment. Barty liked it at Jim's. But Jim hadn't invited him to stay, and they hadn't known each other that long, so he couldn't really expect to be asked to move in or anything. But being home alone sort of sucked. Other people had groups of friends, but Barty had never been able to figure out how to make friends, and yet somehow he'd managed to catch Jim's eye and he'd liked him.

"What are you looking at?" Jim asked from behind him. Barty would have known his voice anywhere.

He smiled and turned away from the window to see a huge bouquet of flowers. "You're here. I wasn't expecting you." His heart did this little excited flippy thing. "What are those for?"

"You," Jim said, handing the huge bundle to him, and Barty stared and then bent to smell them. "I missed you."

"Me too." Barty wanted to set the flowers aside and jump into Jim's arms, but that probably wasn't the best thing to do at this moment. "My apartment seems so empty. Penelope has been pissed off and looking for you ever since we left."

"Is Penelope the only one who's been looking for me?"

"Of course not. I just knew you were busy and didn't want to bother you. The apartment seems small and so empty after spending time at your house."

"And the house seems completely empty and cavernous without you and the princess. So look, I have room, lots of it, and I hate coming home to an empty house. But what I hate more is knowing you're doing the exact same thing. I want you and Penelope to come live at the house. You can have your own room if it will make you feel more comfortable until things get settled between us. I know it's fast, but I know what I want."

"Then why didn't you say anything?" Barty asked.

"Because I don't want to pressure you."

"And I thought you'd want your life back the way it was. I mean, the case was over and… I guess I should have said what I wanted, but it was your house and I didn't feel right asking to stay, and… then I didn't want to go, but I had to… so I did… and it sucked…."

"How about I ask you, then? Barty, I want you to come live with me at my house. Bring Penelope and whatever else you want. That house needs to be filled with life and love, and I want you to help me do that. The last two nights really sucked because you weren't there. I love spending time with you, talking, playing games, watching movies, and just being with you."

"Are you sure?"

"Yes. I love you, and I want to spend as much time with you as I can. I don't want to pressure you, and if you aren't ready to move, I'll understand. But I wanted you to know what I want."

"Me too. I never thought I'd have anyone who'd want me in their life like that."

Jim turned and closed the office door. Then he stalked over to where Barty sat and kissed him hard, pushing the wheeled desk chair back until he bumped the desk. "Now you can't go anywhere." He kissed him again, and Barty wrapped his arms around Jim's neck, holding him tightly. He wanted to do so much more than kiss, but he couldn't allow that here in his office.

"Jim…. We can't here…." Barty's resistance began to crumble, and he wanted more and more with each passing second. He could lock the door, empty his desk, and say to hell with it. "Jim…."

"I know, honey," Jim said, backing away, both of them breathing hard. "Are you ready to go home?"

Barty's lips tingled, and he blinked to try to get his balance once again, but he nodded and gathered his things in his bag, then picked up the flowers. Jim opened the office door, and Barty stepped out to find three of his colleagues watching him. Barty blushed about three shades of red; he could feel the heat in his cheeks and knew what he must look like.

"Having a good time?" Miriam asked, and Barty had no idea what to say.

"I'm going home for the day," Barty finally explained.

"Oh, I see."

"Ma'am, Detective James Crawford," Jim said seriously, and Barty saw Miriam step back. "Barty had some questions that needed to be answered."

Barty kept from laughing until they were in the elevator. "That might have worked if I wasn't carrying these flowers," he said, unable to keep the grin off his face. "Was that one of your games?"

"Sure. She was insinuating that we were in your office having sex. Now, it would have been one thing if that's what we had been doing, but since we weren't, she needed to pay a little."

"But what if she thinks we did anyway?"

"Then she'll think I got really lucky," Jim said and kissed him, pulling away as the door slid open on the ground floor. "Did you drive to work?"

"No. I was going to bike, but I had a flat tire, so I walked. It isn't that far."

Jim took his hand. "Then come on. Let's get some things and Penelope and go home."

Barty followed Jim to his car, and they went the short distance to his apartment. He hurried inside, and Penelope went a little nuts at seeing Jim. Apparently she was as taken with him as Barty was.

"She needs to go in her carrier. She usually has a fit when I try to put her in."

"Like this?" Jim held up the carrier, including cat, and Barty shook his head. "I think she's ready to go."

Barty packed a box of Penelope's things, and Jim took it to the car while Barty packed enough clothes and what he'd need for a few days. He wasn't ready to give up his apartment, in case things went bad or something, but he was ready to go to Jim's.

"What about my car?"

"You can follow me. That way you'll have it. Traffic is going to be heavy, but stay behind me and you'll be just fine." Jim kissed him, and Barty let go of the nervousness and stress that driving always caused him. "Let's get what you want to take into the cars, and we can go. It will take a little while to get home, so be patient."

Jim helped him load what he needed and put Penelope on the floor of the front seat of Barty's car. She cried as soon as Jim closed the door. Barty pulled out of his spot behind Jim and followed him into traffic. He'd always tried to avoid stressful situations, and he was never comfortable driving, but Barty kept an eye on Jim, followed him to the freeway, and stayed right behind him through bumper-to-bumper traffic.

"I know, Penelope. You don't like it in the car, but your crying constantly is not helping me get there any faster. So be quiet and lie down for a while. As soon as I get there, I'll give you some catnip, and you can get as high as a kite if you want." Anything to stop her from crying. Heck, he wished he had some of the dang kitty pot right then. Barty clenched the wheel and leaned forward, driving as carefully as he could until they exited the freeway into the community where Jim lived. The streets were much less congested, and it was much easier going after that. They arrived at Jim's, and Barty pulled into the garage next to Jim's car. He got out and grabbed Penelope's carrier. "She hates me right now."

"It'll be fine." Jim unlocked the door and disabled the alarm, and Barty put the carrier inside and opened it. Penelope zoomed out, took a look at him, then turned away, tail in the air, and headed off into house. "She's so pissed at you."

"Tell me about it." Barty put the carrier in the laundry room and helped Jim bring in the rest of his things. Jim helped him get them upstairs, setting the cases on the floor of the guest room, and maneuvering Barty into his room.

"I hope she'll... oh...." Barty groaned as Jim opened his pants and shoved them down his legs.

"I've missed you."

Barty laughed, and it felt good. "Is this more of your playing? Because if it is, I like it." He wound his arms around Jim's neck to steady himself as he tried to step out of his pants and failed to do so. It would help if he had taken off his shoes.

Jim laughed as Barty nearly tumbled back onto the bed while trying to get out of his damn pants and finally managing it.

"I know you don't love me for my grace and elegance."

"No, honey, I didn't fall in love with you for your grace. It was definitely something else." Jim smiled, looking into his eyes, and Barty went to take off his glasses, but Jim stopped him. "I like your glasses."

"Is that your fetish or something?" Barty asked as Jim made short work of the buttons on his shirt.

"Maybe. I'm not sure. I like tall, intelligent, sort of nerdy guys with glasses, so sue me."

Barty wanted to kiss him instead and did just that. This particular tall, smart, nerdy guy who wore glasses had never expected to find someone. He always thought he never understood other people well enough to catch anyone's eye.

"I guess that proves there's someone for everyone."

"Nope, just that you're the one for me." Jim pressed him back with a kiss that left Barty weak in the knees. Thank goodness he just fell back on the bed, and Jim tugged off the last of his clothes. "Now there's a sight."

"I want to look too, but you're still dressed," Barty said, happy as all get-out at the heat in Jim's eyes. Every time he saw that look, he silently thanked his grandmother. Not that he wanted to be thinking about her when he was naked and Jim was taking off his shirt. Barty tugged at the material, trying to help, and as soon as Jim's chest was exposed, he sat up, put his arms around Jim's waist, and brought his lips to that amazing skin. "I love how strong you are. It makes me feel safe."

Jim stilled. "But...."

"Nope. I always feel safe around you, and I had your back and you have mine." Barty pushed away the image of Mason on the floor. He'd had enough of that. He couldn't stop that from infiltrating his dreams, but it wouldn't interfere with his time with Jim. "That's what matters." He lifted his gaze, gently tugging Jim down until their lips met. The last thing he wanted to talk about now was that bastard—even though he was the reason the two of them were together in the first place. "Nana always said that things happen for a reason, and I got you out of the deal."

"Then I came out a winner," Jim whispered and pressed Barty back onto the bed.

Barty loved the solidity of Jim's weight on him. He'd always hated being held down—the kids had done that to him in school—but this was so different. Jim loved him, and Barty clung as tightly as possible. He didn't want anything to come between them. Of course, Jim had to pull away, if only to get rid of the rest of his clothes.

Jim stood naked at the side of the bed once he'd stripped, and he stared at him. Barty's excitement clicked up a notch each and every second Jim watched him. He wondered what was going on inside his head, and to his surprise, he had no idea whatsoever and loved it. Jim was completely closed to him, and that only added to the anticipation.

Jim pulled open the drawer next to the bed.

"What's that?" Barty asked.

"Something we're going to need a little later." Jim kissed him then climbed on the bed, and Barty forgot about anything else. To say Jim was athletic and full of energy was an understatement. Barty's entire body came alive, picking up on Jim's energy and returning it to him. When Jim kissed him, his head felt like it would explode, and when Jim kissed down his chest and belly, Barty held his breath and clutched the bedding in anticipation. But when Jim straddled him and reached for the things on the nightstand, Barty was a little confused. Jim showed him the condom packet and opened it; then, to Barty's shock, he rolled the condom down Barty's cock, and Barty nearly lost it at the sensation. He still didn't believe what was going to happen. Jim grabbed the lube and slicked him before reaching behind himself. Then, before Barty could really think about it, Jim positioned Barty's cock, and Barty began to slide inside Jim's body.

The sensation was sublime, with heat and pressure building around him. Barty groaned loudly and bit his lower lip, trying not to come so soon because he wanted this to last.

"Just breathe and take it easy," Jim said, continuing to sink down on him until Barty pressed up to meet Jim's butt.

"Jim, this is too much."

"No. It's actually perfect."

"But I thought you...."

"Nope." Jim lifted his hips, and words flew from Barty's head. He forgot about anything else. Jim stroked himself, leaned back, and brought his hips up and down.

Barty wondered if he was ever going to get enough air into his lungs again. The feel of Jim gripping him, the view of Jim stroking his cock, belly clenched, eyes half-lidded—it was better than anything he'd ever seen in any of the movies he'd felt guilty watching. Jim was more beautiful and amazing than anything Barty could have ever imagined, and he wanted Barty just as much as Barty wanted him. That alone added to the excitement.

"I'm...." Barty wasn't sure how long he was going to be able to stay in control. He was over the moon, and Jim pushed all his buttons with the way he clenched around him. That made Barty's eyes roll into the back of his head.

"Almost there," Jim said, stroking faster, belly muscles rolling. Damn, that was hot, and when he clenched, tugging hard at Barty's cock, Barty completely lost it, flying over the precipice of desire with the force of a bullet, lights flashing, muscles tensing, completely out of control.

Barty floated on clouds, and for the first time, knew without a doubt that angels existed, because Jim had moved next to him and held him tightly.

"You're just fine. Keep your eyes closed and relax."

"But...."

"Just be happy. That's all you need to be. Everything else will take care of itself." Jim rubbed small circles on his belly, and Barty realized no one else could possibly make him feel this way. "Are you crying?"

"No," Barty lied and tried not to dry his cheeks.

"Good."

"But what about the next case and the next bad guy? What about…?" He tried not to think about the next person who might want to hurt Jim. "What if I'm not there to watch your back?"

"You'll be there, even when you aren't in the room." Jim kissed him, and Barty knew Jim would be there for him as well. That's what his nana had told him love was: always being there for someone else, no matter what.

Barty closed his eyes and soaked in the warmth of Jim's love, the one thing in life he'd never thought he'd have, and all it had taken was a serial shooter and Barty being willing to work with Jim and play with the gunfire that was part of his life.

# EPILOGUE

BARTY STOOD in the formal living room, staring at the massive real tree that went nearly to the fourteen-foot ceiling. It glittered and glowed with lights and ornaments that Jim's family had been collecting for generations.

"I don't know if I can do this," he said nervously.

"Your family is only coming for Christmas," Jim said from behind him as he climbed a ladder to hang a huge wreath over the fireplace. Jim had wanted a real wreath, so they'd arranged to get it and hang it at the last minute. "This isn't a firing squad. Besides, I'm the one who should be nervous. Your entire family and all the kids are coming here for Christmas."

"You've met them before," Barty said.

"Briefly on a few occasions, but not all of them at the same time." Jim smiled, and Barty knew he was kidding. "The only nervous part is that you insisted that my family come as well for Christmas Eve, including my mother and father." Jim placed the wreath on the hook and then climbed down the ladder and stepped back. "How did you get my mom and dad to agree to come anyway?"

Barty tapped the side of his head. "Psychology."

Jim glared at him.

"Okay, guilt. I told them that you and I were talking about adopting a few children and that if they ever wanted to see their grandchildren, they needed to grow up. Your dad ground his teeth, but your mother wants more grandkids badly enough that she can't stand it so she hushed your father and told me they'd both be there."

Jim put his hands on his hips. "You promised her grandchildren?"

"I said that you and I have talked about adopting, which we have. I purposely didn't give her a timetable."

"Yeah, but now she's going to ask me about it every time I talk to her."

"So? At least she's over the whole gay and being a cop things, which I never understood after catching the bad guy and becoming a sort of local hero. But who knows. People are crazy."

"That coming from the guy who studies crazy."

"Anyway, I didn't lie, and your sister piled on the guilt because she said if they didn't come, then they wouldn't see Mindy and Meghan this Christmas since they're spending Christmas Day with Franklin's family, so they're coming as well."

"So what do we do if they don't get along?"

"The wine chiller in the kitchen is already full. I suggest we pop open a few bottles and let the alcohol flow. Also, I have presents for everyone under the tree so we can always suggest that we open them. That should work. At least it did for Nicole and Mark when they were kids."

"What do you mean, you got presents? You mean extra presents?"

"Well, sort of. I called Deidre, and she helped me with your family, and I got Nicole to help me."

"I thought we were giving gifts together."

"We are, but I got extra gifts and put our names on them. It was fun. By the way, your sister loves to shop." He fanned himself and grinned.

Jim hugged him. "You're a trip, you know that? I'm still trying to figure out how you went from the guy who never played to one of the most fun-loving people I know."

"I think it was the deprivation sort of thing. Once I figured out what I was missing, I think I went a little overboard. You don't mind, do you?"

"Not at all. I like you this way." Jim pulled him closer and kissed him. Barty was about to suggest that they build a fire, get warm, and then really turn up the heat when the doorbell rang and the front door opened.

"Where are you guys?" Deidre called, and soon footsteps raced through the house.

"Uncle Perpy, Uncle Barty," Meghan and Mindy called, and Barty scooped up Mindy while Jim hugged Meghan.

"I knew they'd find you first." Deidre put down the wrapped presents under the tree. "I thought I'd bring these over, and the munchkins insisted on coming."

Barty put Mindy down and hugged Deidre.

178

"I wanted to tell you that if you need any assistance getting your tenure materials together, I can help."

"Oh, it's all done and ready to go. They are apparently so excited about my research that they are developing a special fellowship in order to help fund it. And they loved the idea of a new area of study with economic impact, so our project is a go from their perspective. Basically, once I got that other offer, they couldn't bend over backward far enough to give me whatever I want, and my classes have all filled up, so everything is working out."

"That's so wonderful," Deidre said happily and then turned to where her daughters were playing. "We better get going, girls. Tell your uncles good-bye and that we'll see them the day after tomorrow for Christmas Eve." She turned to Jim. "Are you cooking?"

"I am," Barty said. "I studied up on a lot of holiday dishes, talked to both mothers, figured both yours and mine were crazy, so I came up with my own menu, and everyone is going to love it."

"Okay...."

Jim broke into peals of laughter. "He's kidding. The dinner is being catered. I figured it was safest. But Barty is making the dessert himself."

"Good. I know it's going to be a wonderful time." Deidre hugged them both and then took each of the girls by the hand and led them out of the house.

"Are you really prepared for all this?" Jim asked.

It was Barty's turn to laugh. "We met because I helped you catch a serial shooter, and then I shot the guy after he hit me and was going to shoot you. I think after all that, we can get through a day with all our family." Barty moved once again into the circle of Jim's arms. "Why don't you go lock the doors and set the alarm, and I'll feed the little princess." Who at that moment decided she wanted to sleep on the presents under the tree. "Then we can go on up to our room, and I'll show you just how much I appreciate what you're doing."

Barty kissed him, and then Jim dashed away like he was a little kid ready to open his presents on Christmas morning. The lights went off one by one in the house, and Penelope jumped down from the present she had commandeered and hurried toward the kitchen. Clearly Jim was feeding her.

"You know," Jim said when he returned, the lights off except for the tree. "I think I'm more excited for this Christmas than I have been in a long time." Jim hugged him, and they stood in the middle of the room, looking at the tree. "I got the best present ever this year."

"How do you know? Did you peek?" Deidre had told him that Jim was a huge snoop when it came to presents, and he'd gone to extra effort to hide the ones he'd gotten for Jim.

"No. You're the best present ever." Jim turned him and kissed him right there.

"I love you too," Barty said, and then Jim took him by the hand and they left the room, Jim turning out the tree before leading him upstairs.

DIRK is very much an outside kind of man. He loves travel and seeing new things. Dirk worked in corporate America for way too long and now spends his days writing, gardening, and taking care of the home he shares with his partner of more than two decades. He has a master's degree and all the other accessories that go with a corporate job. But he is most proud of the stories he tells and the life he's built. Dirk lives in Pennsylvania in a century-old home and is blessed with an amazing circle of friends.

Facebook: www.facebook.com/dirkgreyson
E-mail: dirkgreyson@comcast.net

# FLIGHT OR FIGHT

## DIRK GREYSON

Life in the big city wasn't what Mackenzie "Mack" Redford expected, and now he's come home to Hartwick County, South Dakota, to serve as sheriff.

Brantley Calderone is looking for a new life. After leaving New York and buying a ranch, he's settling in and getting used to living at a different pace—until he finds a dead woman on his porch and himself the prime suspect in her murder.

Mack and Brantley quickly realize several things: someone is trying to frame Brantley; he is no longer safe alone on his ranch; and there's a definite attraction developing between them, one that only increases when Mack offers to let Brantley stay in his home. But as their romance escalates, so does the killer. They'll have to stay one step ahead and figure out who wants Brantley dead before it's too late. Only then can they start the life they're both seeking—together.

# www.dreamspinnerpress.com

Day and Knight: Book One

As former NSA, Dayton (Day) Ingram has national security chops and now works as a technical analyst for Scorpion. He longs for fieldwork, and scuttling an attack gives him his chance. He's smart, multilingual, and a technological wizard. But his opportunity comes with a hitch—a partner, Knighton (Knight), who is a real mystery. Despite countless hours of research, Day can find nothing on the agent, including his first name!

Former Marine Knight crawled into a bottle after losing his family. After drying out, he's offered one last chance: along with Day, stop a terrorist threat from the Yucatan. To get there without drawing suspicion, Day and Knight board a gay cruise, where the deeply closeted Day and equally closeted Knight must pose as a couple. Tensions run high as Knight communicates very little and Day bristles at Knight's heavy-handed need for control.

But after drinking too much, Day and Knight wake up in bed. *Together.* As they near their destination, they must learn to trust and rely on each other to infiltrate the terrorist camp and neutralize the plot aimed at the US's technological infrastructure, if they hope to have a life after the mission. One that might include each other.

# www.dreamspinnerpress.com

# DIRK GREYSON
# SUN AND SHADOW

Sequel to *Day and Knight*
Day and Knight: Book Two

Dayton "Day" Ingram is recovering from an injury suffered in Mexico—and from his failed relationship with fellow Scorpion agent, Knight. While researching an old government document, Day realizes he might be holding the key to finding an artistic masterpiece lost since WWII.

But the Russians are looking for it too, and have a team in place in Eastern Europe hunting it down. Day and Knight are brought back together when they are charged with getting to the painting first.

Knight wants to leave Mexico and everything that happened there behind, and return to the life he had—except it wasn't much of a life. When he's partnered up with Day, keeping his distance proves to be challenging. But Day is as stubborn as Knight and isn't willing to let him walk away.

Their assignment leads them through Germany and Austria with agents hot on their tail—agents willing to do whatever it takes to get to the masterpiece first. If Day and Knight can live long enough to find the painting, they might also discover something even more precious—each other.

# www.dreamspinnerpress.com

YELLOWSTONE WOLVES

# CHALLENGE
## *the* DARKNESS

### Dirk Greyson

Yellowstone Wolves: Book One

When alpha shifter Mikael Volokov is called to witness a challenge, he learns the evil and power-hungry Anton Gregor will stop at nothing to attain victory. Knowing he will need alliances to keep his pack together, Mikael requests a congress with the nearby Evergreen pack and meets Denton Arguson, Evergreen alpha, to ask for his help. Fate has a strange twist for both of them, though, and Mikael and Denton soon realize they're destined mates.

Denton resists the pull between them—he has his own pack and his own responsibilities. But Mikael isn't willing to give up. The Mother has promised Mikael his mate, told him he must fight for him, and that only together can they defeat the coming darkness. When Anton casts his sights on Denton's pack, attacks and sabotage follow, pulling Denton and Mikael together to defeat a common enemy. But Anton's threats sow seeds of destruction enough to break any bond, and the mates' determination to challenge the darkness may be their only saving grace.

# www.dreamspinnerpress.com

YELLOWSTONE WOLVES

# DARKNESS THREATENING

## Dirk Greyson

Sequel to *Challenge the Darkness*
Yellowstone Wolves: Book Two

Fredrik is back from college and trying to stay out of his power-hungry brother's way, until his brother takes a prisoner for his pleasure. Unable to tolerate his family's cruelty, Fredrik overcomes his fear to help her escape back to her pack. There, he meets Christopher, and their instant attraction tells him Christopher is the one. However, since the threat of his brother remains, Fredrik is reluctant to pursue a relationship.

Christopher is still figuring out his place in the pack and has been living on his own to avoid making waves with his brother, Mikael. Now he's met his soulmate, and he'll do anything to take care of his love, including rejoining the pack.

With coaxing, Fredrik accepts his feelings, and Christopher's pack gives him the home he's never had. But Fredrick soon realizes he should keep running. His brother is on his tail and will stop at nothing to obtain the power he craves, especially when he realizes the source of the power could be Fredrik himself.

# www.dreamspinnerpress.com

CPSIA information can be obtained
at www.ICGtesting.com
Printed in the USA
BVOW08s1917140917
494784BV00010B/217/P